Night

with a

SEAL

Cat Johnson

ACKNOWLEDGMENTS

I could not have created the characters in this series without having read *No Easy Day* written by Mark Owen with Kevin Maurer. This autobiography of a SEAL provided me with a glance into the minds, attitudes and characters of the men who sign up for this challenging life. It also would not be the story it is without the eagle eyes of my personal military consultants who check for the civilian mistakes I make. That said, any mistakes or liberties taken with the facts are purely my own.

CHAPTER ONE

The glare of the sun bounced off the hood as Jon steered his truck to the curb and parallel parked in front of his buddy's place. Cutting the engine, he evaluated the house through the dark lenses of his sunglasses. It was nice for a rental. He'd definitely lived in worse. They all had.

He stepped out of the air-conditioned cab of the vehicle and pocketed the keys. It was hot outside, but not unbearable considering it was summer in Virginia. He'd take sunny and high eighties any day rather than the hundred-and-twenty degrees Fahrenheit that would be waiting for him in Afghanistan.

Jon moved around to open the passenger door and grab the cold eighteen-pack from the floor. It was going to be a good day. He had cold beer, good friends and Rick had promised them some tasty barbecue.

Best of all, he was actually stateside for a holiday. It was only Fourth of July—not one of the big days like Thanksgiving or Christmas, both of which he'd spent deployed last year—but it was a federal holiday so officially it counted.

He made his way up the short path to the front door and, case of beer in his hands, hit the doorbell with his elbow.

It was a nice change, walking up to a door in daylight and ringing the bell rather than creeping through the dark wearing night vision goggles and blowing the lock. It was the little things such as being able to approach a door and not have to dodge automatic gunfire that a man grew to appreciate after a decade of combat deployments.

The door swung wide and all six-foot-five of Rick Mann's hulking frame filled the opening. Built like a linebacker, Rick always had made Jon— whose six-foot-two-inch frame was lean muscle rather than bulk—feel small.

"Dude, good to see you." Jon held the beer with his left arm and clasped right hands with his former teammate.

"You too. I never thought I'd say this, but I actually miss seeing that smartass face of yours all hours of the day and night." Rick grinned and stepped back to let Jon inside the front door of the house. "Come on in. The party's going to be around back on the deck."

As Rick led the way through the house, Jon glanced around him. It wasn't huge, but it was neat and comfortable. A big flat-screen TV hung on one wall of the living room. Just past the living room furniture was an island lined with stools and a decent sized kitchen with appliances that looked to be fairly new.

Except for an overabundance of floral throw pillows covering the sectional sofa and the room's two upholstered chairs—a clear sign Rick lived with a female—a man could be very happy kicking back here.

Jon tipped up his chin and called a greeting to Rick's sister Darci in the kitchen. With a phone pressed to her ear, she smiled and wiggled her fingers in a wave.

"Nice digs," Jon said as he skirted around a dining table and chair on his way to the sliding glass doors.

Rick let out a huff. "Thanks."

He'd sounded less than enthusiastic and as Rick glanced over his shoulder, Jon saw his scowl. "What's the face for? I meant it."

Rick made a face again. "You know this is Darci's place."

"Yeah. So?" Jon asked. "It's still nice."

"I just never thought I'd be living with family at this point in my life. Moving in with my little sister is barely a step up from moving back home with my parents."

"Hey, it's not a big deal." Jon shrugged. "You only got out a couple of months ago. And it didn't make sense to buy your own place while you were active duty."

Rick's brow rose. "You bought yours."

"Yup." Jon nodded. "And I'm there less than half the months of the year, but even so, the bills still keep coming every damn month, so who's the smart one here? You are."

It had made sense for Rick to live in the bachelor quarters on base for the months their squad was stateside, and then just move his stuff into storage for the months they were deployed. It would be logical for Jon to do the same, except that he rarely did what was logical.

Besides, Jon liked coming home to a turnkey condo that was all his. It was far better than being at the mercy of base housing, which had left more than a few guys without a room after returning home from deployment. Real nice welcome home, that.

Team members without family in the area usually crashed on Jon's sofa until a room became available for them. Sometimes it took a few days, sometimes a couple of weeks, but Jon didn't mind the company. At this point, he and the guys spent so much time together he was more comfortable being with them than apart.

"I guess." Rick continued to look miserable as he yanked open the sliding glass door leading onto the back deck.

Rick was obviously experiencing the grass-is-always-greener syndrome. Jon had seen it before. Guys who were in the military dreamed about getting out, while at the same time guys who'd gotten out lamented about how much better things were when they'd been in.

SEALs were no different than any regular Joe in that respect.

"I've got a cooler full of ice in the shade under the tree. You can put the beer in there." Rick tipped his head toward the cooler and then reached to raise the cover on a stainless steel barbecue grill. "I gotta check the ribs real quick."

"Sounds good."

Ribs. That explained the tantalizing scent he'd smelled wafting from the closed grill when they'd stepped outside. Jon sniffed the meat-laden air as he made his way down the steps and across the lawn.

The yard was nice. Small enough to be easy to keep up, but private thanks to a fence and some well-placed landscaping. So far, Jon saw nothing for Rick to be complaining about. Living here, Rick should be a lot happier than he appeared to be. But to each his own.

Kneeling in the grass, Jon paused while tearing open the cardboard case. He breathed in the scent of freshly mowed lawn that hit him now that he was away from the smoke of the grill.

Never mind taking time to smell the roses, after spending so much time in the desert even just the sight of a patch of lush green grass could stop Jon in his tracks. He ran his hands over the shorn blades and felt them tickle his palm. It might be one of the last opportunities he'd have to appreciate things like backyard grass.

The squad couldn't tell anyone the exact timing, but barring any last minute changes Jon's unit would be heading back to the sandbox next week to spend the remainder of the year in the war zone.

Summer in Afghanistan sucked. But then again, so did winter. . . and the rainy season. . . and fighting season.

Jon had to think that Rick didn't know how good he had it.

Catching himself in a grass-is-always-greener

moment, he focused back on his task—stowing the beer in the ice.

When he got to the last couple of bottles, he closed the lid and carried two longnecks back to the deck. He handed one to Rick, trying not to let his mouth water at the scent of the meat grilling just feet away.

That was another thing he wasn't looking forward to—what passed as food in the chow halls of Jalalabad.

Jon pushed that thought out of his mind and glanced at the near dozen or so folding chairs scattered around the deck and lawn. "Who all are you expecting?"

"Darci invited one of her girlfriends from work. Brody and Chris just called from the car. They're on the way over. Grant's coming with his wife and Thom has his kids today so he's bringing them, but get this...Zane asked if he could bring a date."

"Did he?" Jon's eyes widened. The week before a deployment was a hell of a time to get involved with a new chick. "Wow. I wonder if it's that girl he was talking about before the meeting the other day. The one he hooked up with at the bar after the shooting range last week."

"I don't know." Rick's unhappy expression caught Jon's eye.

Jon reviewed what he could have said to get Rick pissed off and realized that of course Rick hadn't been at the team meeting or the range or the bar.

He and Rick would always be friends, no matter what. They'd been together since BUD/S. Surviving something that hard together formed lifelong bonds that could never be broken. Jon had no doubt of that, but Rick leaving the team meant he wouldn't be there for a lot of things from now on.

Time for Jon to change the subject. "How's the new job going?"

Rick shrugged. "It's all right."

"Just all right?" Jon cocked a brow.

"I sit on my ass and watch monitors to make sure no crazy assholes try to blow up the nuclear power plant, so yeah, it's just all right."

"That doesn't sound so bad." Jon tried to sound upbeat while in his head he was thinking that with his attention deficit disorder he'd probably lose his mind if he had to do Rick's job. Jon needed action. Even the downtime on missions got to him.

"It doesn't?" Letting out a snort, Rick shook his head. "I'm bored out of my freaking mind and I swear I can feel my muscles atrophying just from sitting for so many hours a day."

Jon laughed. "Yeah, I guess if nothing else the Navy does keep us in good shape."

Rick let out a short bitter laugh. "I didn't appreciate how much until now."

"You able to run yet?" Jon asked, eyeing the scar from the surgery on Rick's knee.

"Yeah. I can't push too hard, but I've been trying to put in a few miles every day."

Another touchy subject—the recurring knee issues that had finally pushed Rick to give the civilian world a try. Ten years in the military had beat the hell out of his body. More than half of those years had been spent surviving the escalated physical demands all SEALs were subjected to,

7

those in DEVGRU especially. The Navy's Special Warfare Development Group selection and nine-month training course made BUD/S look like a cakewalk.

Jon needed to come up with some better small talk because so far he'd done nothing but raise topics that upset his former teammate.

Brody walking around the side of the house with a watermelon on his shoulder and his older brother Chris, directly behind him carrying a case of beer, was a welcome interruption to this conversation. Jon raised his bottle and called a greeting to the Cassidy brothers, happy for the distraction not just for Rick's sake but also for his own.

They could both use a break from the subject of Rick's post-military blues, and Chris the jokester and Brody the philosopher were just the two to provide it—at least until Zane showed up with his mystery date. Then they'd all have that as a distraction because knowing Zane she'd be something to look at. Likely not much to talk to but even so, this was going to be an interesting day.

CHAPTER TWO

"Where are you? Why aren't you here yet?"

Alison rolled her eyes at the near panic she heard in Darci's voice. "Relax. I'm in the car and on my way. I had to wait for the boiled potatoes to cool before I could finish making the salad I'm bringing."

"Oh, okay. That's all right then. I love your potato salad."

She laughed at her best friend's priorities. Food always was high on the list, and even so, Darci remained a size four. Meanwhile, Ali starved herself and still was a curvy size ten, sometimes a twelve. Though, she had been known to squeeze herself into a size eight on occasion, if the cut was right and there was plenty of stretch in the fabric.

"So how far away are you?" Darci asked.

"I don't know. Not too far. What's the big hurry?" Ali was on her way to a Fourth of July barbecue, not trying to catch a flight at the airport.

"A bunch of Rick's friends are here already."

Ali glanced at the clock on the dashboard. "It's barely even two yet. I thought that's when you said to come over."

"I know, but from what I've seen, SEALs are never late. Not even the retired ones."

Ali still didn't see the need to rush. It wasn't like she was the one bringing the appetizers, or more importantly the beer. *Then* Darci might have reason to panic. Ali could imagine that Darci's brother could easily freak out if he'd invited all his Navy buddies over and there wasn't any beer when they arrived.

To appease her friend, Ali said, "I'll be there in a couple of minutes."

"Good. There's someone I want you to meet."

The reason for Darci's persistence was suddenly very apparent to Ali. "Um, no."

"Why not?"

"Because I told you I don't want to be fixed up with anybody." Ali scowled at the mere thought.

"I think you'll change your mind once you meet him. Dark hair. Cut muscles. Six-foot-two and eyes of blue."

"So now we're rhyming? Stop. It's creepy. You're like some weird cross between Dr. Seuss and the Millionaire Matchmaker."

Darci let out a laugh. "Well, Rick and his friends certainly aren't millionaires, but they are hot. I can promise you that. The US Navy churns out men with some of the hardest bodies you've ever seen. And I don't mean like those pumped up steroid-filled monsters you find at the gym. These guys are in seriously good shape. They work them until they're completely exhausted to simulate the stress of combat."

"How do you know all this?" Ali frowned. "I thought all this SEAL stuff was top secret."

"Pfft. Thanks to the media, there's not much that stays secret for long nowadays. Besides, that Rick had to do hundreds of sit-ups and push-ups and stuff like that when he was active isn't exactly classified information. I mean who cares if the enemy knows our guys are in tip-top condition? That should only make them think twice about trying anything. Right?"

"I guess." What did Ali know about national security? Not much, that's what. But she did know her friend was as single as she was, which raised a good question. "So if they're so hot, why aren't you dating one of them?"

"I can't date one of Rick's teammates. I know them too well. They're like brothers to me. Before he got out, Rick was with these guys practically twenty-four-seven."

That brought up another question—or more an objection disguised in the form of a question. Alison remembered just last year when Rick was still in the military and he disappeared. He not only hadn't told Darci where he was or what he was doing, he also didn't respond to any of her attempts to contact him. For weeks. Darci had absolutely flipped out, convinced he was dead and the Navy just hadn't told her and their parents yet.

To this day Darci didn't know where he'd been.

Security was that tight. Ali wasn't sure she was up for that kind of stress in a relationship. Dating a nice boring normal guy was hard enough without the challenges of operational security thrown in.

"This guy you're so hot to set me up with, is he still in the military or is he out like your brother?"

Not having come from a military background, it was very odd for her to be talking about guys just a few years older than herself as having retired from their career, even if Rick had gotten out early because of his knee issues. But like Darci said, the life of a SEAL was rough, which she supposed made it a younger man's game. No different than being a top professional athlete, she guessed.

"He's still active duty," Darci answered.

Ali let out a frustrated huff. "Forget about it. Now I'm *really* not interested. I'm not about to get seriously involved with a guy who's away all the time on secret missions. I have a bad enough track record with men who actual stay put."

"Fine, then don't start anything long term. Have a fling instead."

"I can't do that." Ali's voice squeaked over Darci's suggestion.

"Why not? I sure as hell won't judge you."

Darci better not judge. In the two years they'd worked together at the bank, Ali had acted as Darci's wingman for more than a few of her friend's hook-ups.

Alison didn't mention that and moved right on to answering the question. "I'm not going to have a fling with him because I'm sure Navy SEALs have so many women who want to sleep with them, they have to beat them all off with a stick. I am not going to get in that line just so I can be another notch in one of their belts."

Thanks to the military installations at Dam Neck and Little Creek, being anywhere in this part of Virginia meant that the bars were always full of women looking for SEALs and men, both Navy and civilian, taking advantage of that fact.

"Just please, Ali. Keep an open mind until you meet Jon. Okay?"

"Okay." At least Ali knew his name now. She'd know to avoid this Jon during the barbecue before Darci embarrassed them both by blatantly throwing them together.

"So how close are you now?" Darci asked, still sounding a bit too enthusiastic for Ali's arrival.

God, save her from well meaning friends. Ali sighed. "Relax. I'm on your street, and if you let me get off the phone so I can park the car, I'll get there even faster."

"Good. Hurry up." Darci disconnected the call while Ali drew in a bracing breath and prepared for what would greet her at this party.

Sometimes being single was too much work, especially amid do-gooder friends trying to play matchmaker.

Ali pulled up to park behind a truck so large her fuel-efficient economy car almost fit beneath it. No doubt it belonged to one of these SEALs Darci was so hot for Ali to meet. While these guys were off saving the world, they should probably also consider the environment and the impact their gas-guzzlers had on it.

As Ali flipped down the visor she shook her head, mad first at Darci and then at herself for feeling the need to check her hair and make up before she went inside.

This barbecue had gone from low key to stressful in the span of one phone call. She even began to second-guess her outfit. The sundress showed enough skin to make her look like she was inviting male attention, when in reality she'd worn it because of the heat. The same reason she'd put her hair up instead of leaving it down for the day.

Too late to change anything now. She slid her sunglasses on—they'd be a good shield so she could unobtrusively observe the others and avoid eye contact—and opened the door. Time to face the music. . . or at least her interfering friend and some SEALs.

Ali walked around the car and was almost to the path before she remembered to grab the potato salad out of the trunk. Darci's phone call had her all distracted, and for nothing too because there was no way she was going to fall for or have a fling with one of the guys here today.

That resolve firmly in place, she strode to the front doorstep, where she had to work to balance the plastic container filled with potato salad between her arm and hip so she could hit the doorbell.

"Need a hand?" The deep, masculine voice startled her.

Ali jumped and nearly fumbled the very container she'd been struggling not to drop. She hadn't seen the guy come around the corner of the house. He'd stalked silently across the grass like a ninja or, she supposed, a SEAL.

"Um, no, I got it. I just was having trouble ringing the bell."

"No need. The party's right around back. And since it looks like you're bringing food, I'm sure you'll be welcome." He grinned. "You are here for Rick's party, right?"

"Yeah, but at Darci's invitation actually. I brought the potato salad." Ali held up the container unnecessarily. She seriously sucked when it came to making small talk with hot guys.

"I love potato salad." He stepped closer and reached to grab the plastic container from her. "You make it with mayo or vinegar?"

His determination told her he was taking the container whether she wanted him to or not, so she relinquished her hold and let him as she said, "Both, actually. Mostly mayo with a little vinegar. And a little mustard and just a dash of cayenne."

Jeez. Now she was babbling and about recipes of all things. Why didn't she just tell him how long she'd boiled the potatoes for too? Ali stifled a groan at her own ineptitude.

"Really?" His brows rose. "Wow. That sounds really good. I can't wait to try it. You must be Darci's friend from work."

"I am."

Standing as close as they were, his height dwarfed Ali as he smiled down at her. "I'm Jon, a friend of Rick's."

This was Jon? Crap. Darci had been right. He was cute. She couldn't see the *eyes of blue* past his dark sunglasses, but the rest lived up to what Darci had promised. "Nice to meet you. I'm Ali."

The front door of the house opening startled Ali for the second time in a matter of minutes. She glanced over to see Darci beaming. "Ali. Hi. I see you two have met."

"Yup. Jon and I have met." Ali widened her eyes to let Darci in on the fact she knew exactly who the guy in possession of her salad was.

Jon tipped his head toward the road and said to Darci, "I was just running out to my truck to grab the wire so we could hook Rick's phone to the stereo when I saw Ali struggling. Here, I'll give you this back now."

Ali took the container and watched him shoot her one more brilliant smile before he stepped down the front stairs and toward—as she'd suspected—the big pick-up truck.

Funny, she didn't feel as judgmental about his lack of a fuel-efficient vehicle now that she'd met him.

"So?" Darci was visibly bubbling over with excitement as she backed up to give Ali room to go inside.

"He's very nice." It was all she could do to disguise how she was about to melt just from two minutes with the man. Cute. Hot. Polite. Jon seemed to be the whole package.

"You are such a liar." Darci scowled.

"What?" Ali did her best to sound innocent as she followed Darci through the house.

"You can't hide it from me. You're interested, so stop trying to pretend."

"Okay, fine. He's very good looking, just like

you said."

"Thank you." Darci delivered a satisfied nod as she took the container from Ali and turned toward the fridge.

Ali glanced out the kitchen window. "Sounds like quite a few guys are here already."

"Some. Chris and Brody arrived a few minutes ago. The others should be coming any minute."

"And why are you so hot to fix me up with Jon in particular? What's wrong with all these other guys? Are they not single?" Suspicious, Ali had to wonder at Darci's focus on this one guy, not that she was complaining. She just liked to have all the necessary information.

"Why?" Darci slipped the container on to the shelf of the fridge and then turned back to Ali, frowning. "Don't you like Jon? He's so nice—"

"He is very nice." And hot. . . "I didn't say he wasn't. Just answer the question, Miss Evasive."

"I'm not being evasive. In my expert opinion, Jon's the best choice for you."

That *expert opinion* was up for debate, considering the last guy who Darci had decided was perfect for Ali. She shivered just thinking about how badly that blind date had turned out.

Ali crossed her arms and leveled her gaze at her friend as she waited for her answer.

Finally, Darci huffed out a breath. "Fine. Here's the run down. My brother is no good because I can see there's no spark between you two. And considering we're friends, that would be a big mess if you two dated and then broke up."

Ali nodded. "I agree. Next."

Darci rolled her eyes. "Grant's married. You'll meet him and his wife today. The other guys are single, but Thom is divorced with two little kids and you don't want that kinda baggage. Zane is freaking gorgeous, but he's a total ladies man and he's bringing a date today anyway, so he's out. Chris is the joker of the group even though he's the oldest of them all and I'm not convinced he can be serious about anything, never mind a relationship. If he could be, he'd have been married long before now. Then there's Brody. He can get a little dark and broody sometimes."

"Brody is broody. Got it." Ali's head spun with the names and information Darci had ticked off on her fingers, but she didn't worry that she would never keep them all straight because it didn't matter anyway. She wasn't going to date any one of them.

"Obviously, Jon's the only logical one, so do you like him?"

It wasn't quite so obvious to Ali, but Darci looked like a kid on Christmas morning waiting for the answer.

Ali shrugged. "Like I said, he seems nice."

That was all the encouragement Ali was willing to give. She was here to enjoy a cold beverage and some good food on her day off. Not to partake of the man buffet Darci had listed for her, even with how good the first dish she'd come across had looked.

CHAPTER THREE

Jon pulled the wire out of his truck's dashboard audio input and carried it back to the house, only to notice the very attractive brunette and her potato salad had already gone inside.

Having his new acquaintance to look at during today's gathering would be no hardship. Pretty in pink in her floral sundress, Ali was like a breath of fresh air on the hot July day. Jon should really thank Darci later for inviting her. It was nice that Rick's barbecue wouldn't be the usual sausage fest.

Not that Jon would take advantage of that and act upon this chance meeting with the woman. They were counting down in hours now, rather than days, until the squad left for a solid six months overseas. Bad timing, if ever he saw it.

Keeping that in mind, he cut across the lawn and made his way around the house.

"Got it?" Rick asked as Jon bounded up the

stairs to the deck.

"I do." Jon handed over the small white connector that he used to plug his smartphone into his truck's audio so he could listen to his own music rather than the radio.

"Perfect. Thanks. Now we can have some decent tunes." Rick moved toward the house.

Darci, coming out, stopped in the doorway just in time to hear the discussion about music. "I can go and get my iPod if you want."

"Um, no. I've heard what's on yours. We're using mine." Rick pushed past Darci and into the house as she turned and followed him.

Jon smiled as the siblings continued to bicker all the way into the house, before his attention turned to Ali, who'd walked out of the door with bowls of chips and dip in her hands.

She set them on the table and cut her gaze sideways to him. "Do they fight like this often?"

He let out a laugh. "Yeah. Pretty much every time I've seen them together."

Not that he saw them together all that often. Time with family was pretty limited in his line of work. One reason why he was single. He reminded himself of that as he realized that he could see a distracting amount of Ali's cleavage from this angle. He reached out and grabbed a chip to distract himself.

Music—hard acid metal—came blaring out of the house. Jon recognized it as one of the songs from the playlist Rick listened to for PT. The music screeched to a sudden halt during which Jon was sure the sibling battle continued inside. The silence lasted a few more seconds before a country tune came on, still a selection he recognized from one of Rick's work out playlists, but far more mellow.

Apparently they'd reached a compromise. He smiled as he raised the bottle to his lips.

"So Darci says you're deploying again soon." Ali's question brought his head around to her.

If she wanted small talk, he could do small talk. Though he did find it interesting that Darci and Ali had been discussing his squad, considering Rick was no longer a part of it.

"Yup." Jon kept the response brief and indefinite, not giving anything away. After all these years, he was an expert at answering questions without really answering them.

"Are you worried?" A small wrinkle creased the space between her brows.

"Worried? Nah. This'll be my thirteenth combat deployment."

"Thirteen." She cringed and then hid the expression as she glanced at him.

Jon frowned at her reaction. "What's wrong?"

"Nothing." Eyes visibly widening behind her sunglasses, she tried to look innocent and failed.

Realization hit him and he laughed. "Are you concerned about this being my thirteenth?"

"You're not?" She sounded skeptical.

"No, I'm not. Believe me, of all the many things that could kill me, kill us all really on a daily basis, the number thirteen is pretty low on the list." He took a sip of his beer and eyed the brunette. "Are you superstitious?"

"I've been known to knock wood on occasion,

and I do firmly believe Karma's a bitch." She let out a short laugh. "Do you think less of me now?"

"Not at all. But I do think less of myself that I'm letting you stand here in the hot sun and haven't even offered to get you something cold to drink. What's your pleasure?" Jon wrangled his mind off the many pleasures they could share together if things were different. He moved on to list for her the different drinks he'd seen in the cooler.

"I'll have a beer, I guess."

He raised his bottle to her in a toast. "A woman after my own heart. Stay right here. I'll be back."

By the time Jon got down the stairs, Rick was already at the cooler sticking bottles of water into the ice. Rick glanced up at him as Jon reached past and grabbed a bottle of beer. "So, I saw you talking to Darci's friend."

If there was a question buried in there, Jon didn't hear it. Even so, he nodded. "Yup."

"Do you like her?" Rick's expression seemed to light up. Why, Jon didn't know.

Even if Jon was the type to get serious with a girl, which he wasn't, he sure as hell wasn't going to do it on what could literally be the eve of a six month deployment that would drop him directly into the armpit of the war zone.

When they packed all their gear in three days— or tomorrow or the next day for all he knew—he needed his head to be firmly in the game, not on some piece of ass back in the States waiting on him.

Zane came out of the house and onto the deck at that moment. Jon saw Zane's own bad decision hanging on his arm like he was a buoy and she was in open seas. It worked to cement Jon's resolve on the matter. No relationships for him. At least not now.

Jon wrestled his attention away from squinting through his sunglasses at Zane's date. He'd been trying to determine if she was the same girl he'd seen riding a pole at the strip club in town last time he'd been dragged there by the guys.

He turned to Rick and finally answered the man's question. "I don't know if I like her or not. I just met her. Why are you so concerned about me and Ali?"

Rick shrugged. "No reason. Just wondering."

Apparently civilian life and boredom had turned Rick into a busybody. "Have another beer. You can't be called in anymore. You can get as drunk as you want, so go for it."

Jon, on the other hand, had to throttle his own consumption. Even on an official "day off", they still had to be mission ready on a moment's notice. All of their pagers could go off at any time, and then they'd have to be at base and ready to go within an hour. He had become an expert on exactly how many drinks he could metabolize and still be okay if he got called in—just another of the many skills he'd picked up over the years.

It was good he couldn't get sloppy drunk though, because a few too many often led to poor decisions. Thom came around the corner with his two kids and cemented Jon's resolve further. Little Tommy had been conceived during a night when Thom forgot how much he could consume safely, which had led to the unplanned pregnancy and as a result the failed marriage he'd just signed the papers to end.

Rick's snort brought Jon's attention back to him. "I'd rather be deploying with the squad, than getting drunk here."

"I know, buddy. I know." Jon slapped his friend on the back and tipped his head toward the house. "Let's go get a closer look at Zane's date, shall we?"

If she was indeed who he thought she was, Jon wondered what name she was going by here. He rarely forgot a face—or any other body part—and he doubted she'd be using her stripper name, Mistress Mona, here at the barbecue. Then again, who knew?

Throttling down in concession to the heat and the fact his belly was empty and grumbling thanks to the barbecue on the horizon, Jon grabbed a bottle of water for himself and carried it to the deck along with Ali's beer.

Grant had arrived at some point while Jon had been talking to Rick. He came out of the house now, his wife carrying a platter of what looked to be cheese and crackers.

The small roster of attendees was complete, but there was only one person Jon made a beeline for after climbing the stairs. He told himself it was because he had the beer he'd promised her, but deep down he knew that adorable little frown over the number thirteen coupled with the very attractive cleavage she was sporting had long since won him over.

Too bad a one-night stand was out of the

question given who she was, and he didn't do long term.

Maybe Ali had been correct. Karma, being a bitch, had dropped the smoking hot friend of his best friend's sister in his path right before a deployment. If that wasn't cosmic payback for his sins, he didn't know what it was. After all the shit he'd done in the name of God and country while fighting an enemy who claimed the same, he supposed a larger neutral presence—if one existed—could find plenty to judge him on.

She was facing away from him, talking to Darci and Grant's wife, Molly. He tapped Ali on the shoulder and thrust the bottle toward her when she turned.

"Thanks." The smile she sent him was enough to make him silently curse Fate one more time.

CHAPTER FOUR

"Are you sure you're okay to drive?" Darci's asked.

"I'm fine. I had like three beers over the course of five hours on top of so much food I doubt my pants for work will fit in the morning." Ali dismissed her friend's concern with the wave of one hand while she cradled her clean, empty container from the long gone potato salad with the other.

Cell phone in his hand, Rick walked up to the conversation happening right inside the front door. "Grant just called. He wanted to warn everybody. He just drove through a drunk driving checkpoint."

Darci's eyes widened. "Is he okay?"

"Oh, yeah. Molly was driving and she hadn't had anything at all to drink. He was just worried because they're really cracking down for the holiday and some of the guys have had a couple."

Darci spun back to Ali. "I think you should stay

the night."

"Darci. I'm fine, and we have work in the morning." It sucked that the Fourth of July provided for only one day off but in the age of twenty four / seven customer service she supposed she should be lucky to get even that anymore.

"I'll take her home." The deep voice coming from behind Rick heralded Jon's joining the conversation.

Ali's heart knocked against her ribcage at hearing Jon's offer. "Then my car will be here. And isn't there no street parking overnight? I'll get a ticket."

"No, you won't. I'll move your car into the driveway as soon as it's clear tonight. And I'll pick you up in the morning. You can get it tomorrow after work." Darci's solution was going to make it impossible for Ali to get out of being alone with this tempting man offering her a ride home.

Ali had managed to keep Darci from throwing them together during the party, but she hadn't quite managed to control herself. All throughout those five hours she kept finding herself glancing to see where he was. Turning at the sound of his laugh. Noticing the flex of his muscles as he helped Rick carry the cooler up the stairs once the sun had moved behind the trees to shade the deck.

Being with him, in his truck, at her door, would be too damn tempting. "Thanks for offering, but you don't have to do that."

"It's no trouble. Really."

"But you don't even know where I live."

He shrugged. "I'm assuming it can't be too far."

"It's not. Ten minutes, max." Darci jumped in and dispelled Ali's last objection.

"That's nothing. I can drop you off." Jon's brilliant blue eyes, framed by the tan line left from his sunglasses, pinned her with such intensity that she felt like she had to agree.

She held in her sigh. It seemed there was no fighting this. She handed over the car keys in her hand to Darci. "Okay. Thank you, Jon."

"No problem." Bottle of water in his left hand, Jon turned and extended his right to Rick. "Dude, thanks for a great party."

"You're welcome. Hey, keep in touch. Okay?"

"You got it." Jon dipped his head.

Rick's last comment felt heavy as he held Jon's hand for a bit longer than necessary for a casual handshake between friends. It almost sounded like a final goodbye and Ali realized since Jon was deploying, it could be—at least for the next few months, if not for forever.

That thought stuck with Ali as she and Jon made their way through the deepening shadows of the path toward his truck. He leapt forward to open the door before she reached it, and took the container from her while she grabbed the handle inside and hoisted herself into the high truck.

"Thanks."

"Sure." He smiled when he handed the plastic tub back to her, and then walked around to the driver's side. That gave her time to recover from the effect his intense gaze had on her now that it was evening and he'd taken his sunglasses off.

Jon was the kind of man who opened doors for a

28

lady. . . and he was shipping off to war. For every pro, there was an equal and opposite con. Yup, that sounded about right as far as Ali's usual bad luck in the man department.

He fired up the big engine and pulled smoothly away from the curb, leaving her little car behind them. When he stopped in the middle of the street, and turned his head to look at her, she waited, wondering what the hold up was.

He finally asked, "Which way should I go?"

"Oh, sorry." She'd forgotten to tell him. Jeez, she was a mess. "Head out to the main road at the end of this street. I'm a couple of miles past the Big Mart shopping center."

He nodded. "Got it."

Renewed guilt for putting him out had her angling in her seat to face him. "I really could have driven."

"I know, but why take a chance?" He shrugged.

"I guess. Thank you again."

The corner of his mouth lifted in a smile as his eyes remained focused on the road ahead. "You're welcome. Again."

"So I guess you'll be leaving soon. To deploy." Maybe she had consumed too much to drive. Considering how ridiculously bad her attempt at small talk was, that had to be the reason.

"Most likely." He dipped his head in a nod.

"I just wanted to apologize for Darci." Sucky conversational skills or not, Ali still wanted that out there. Ali had to make sure Jon knew it was Darci trying to set them up and that it hadn't been her idea.

"Apologize for what?"

"She had this crazy idea to fix us up. Of course, I set her straight but she was still kind of obvious about it." Ali wouldn't be surprised if Darci had engineered the whole police check scenario with Rick just to get her in the car with Jon.

"Why of course?" He shot her a look from across the spacious cab.

"Excuse me?"

"You said that *of course* you set her straight. Why of course?"

"Well, because you're about to leave the country for who knows how long. It would be crazy to try and start anything."

"You're right. It would be." He nodded, his tone giving nothing away so she couldn't tell if he was surprised by her words or not. "What did she say when you told her that?"

Ali felt her cheeks heat. When she hesitated answering, he turned his head to her.

"What's wrong? What did she say?" Jon repeated the question.

"That we should just have a fling instead." Unable to come up with a lie on the fly, Ali opted for the truth, but then laughed as if it was a big joke rather than an idea that had her insides twisting.

Out of the corner of her eye, she saw his brow rise as he asked, "What did you say to that suggestion?"

Was his voice huskier than before? No. It was probably just her imagination. Even so, her heart rate sped. Not believing they were actually having this conversation, she swallowed hard and said,

"That I couldn't do that."

"No. You're not the one-night stand type." Not sure whether to take his comment as an insult or a compliment, Ali frowned.

"Well, no. I haven't been in the past." With her bad judgment when it came to men firmly in place, she decided she wouldn't mind being that type now. "Besides, you SEALs probably have dozens of women throwing themselves at you day and night. . ."

Pure unadulterated lust was the best excuse she could come up with for her continuing this conversation about one-night stands with Jon.

He let out a short laugh. "Not quite as many women as you'd think."

"I'm not sure I believe you." She remembered Zane's well-endowed date at the party.

Jon shrugged. "I don't go out all that much and aside from my cleaning lady, there's no women hanging around my condo."

"Oh." Crap. She wanted this man. Good thing he didn't want her.

His lack of interest came through clearly in the flat tone of his questions and answers. At least one of them was thinking clearly. Her long dry spell in the sexual encounter department would surely lead them down a dangerous path if things had been left solely up to her.

"We just passed the shopping center."

"Oh, um sorry. Make a right at the next light." Her cheeks heated again as she looked like an idiot for forgetting to tell him where to go. Ali wrestled her attention off her burning desire for this man and onto the road as he flipped on the blinker and made the turn. "Then it's a right at the stop sign."

He nodded and followed her directions right up to the driveway of the duplex she rented. It was dark since she hadn't left any lights on when she'd left this afternoon but Jon's headlights would light her way to the door.

She'd get to the door fine. That wasn't the issue. The problem was that she knew it was locked and the key was with her car keys she'd left with Darci.

"Crap." Ali let out the curse beneath her breath when she realized the full impact of what she'd done.

"Problem?" he asked.

"You're not going to believe this." Ali forced herself to look at him, even though she was so embarrassed she felt her cheeks warm.

He cocked one brow. "Try me."

"My house key is on the ring with my car keys—"

He nodded as an expression of comprehension dawned. "At Rick's place."

"Yup." Now she really did look like a complete idiot.

Jon reached for the handle and swung the door wide. Where he thought he was going Ali didn't know, but as he rounded the hood and came to open her door it appeared she'd be going with him.

"The door's locked." She felt the need to clarify that point since judging by his actions her tale of the absent keys hadn't seemed to resonate with him. He strode for the door and tried the knob as she came up behind him.

"Yeah, I figured. Just checking." He turned to glance at her. "You have a back door?"

"Yes." Which would be locked too but she had a feeling he was going to want to check anyway.

"Okay. Wait here."

She was about to tell him she was absolutely certain that door was locked, but he was too fast as he jogged around the dark corner of the building.

Crossing her arms, she figured she'd hang out and wait. It would only be a matter of time before he was back and they'd have to face the fact they'd have to go all the way back to Darci's to retrieve her keys. Embarrassment heated her cheeks at the thought. As if it weren't enough of an imposition that he'd had to drive her home, now he'd have to do it twice.

The sound of the lock turning right before the front door swung in had Ali turning wide-eyed to see Jon smiling in the doorway. He took a step back and swept one arm. "Would you like to come in?"

"How—" She shook her head, at a loss for words.

He grinned wider. "Lock picking is just one of my many skills."

"Does the Navy teach you guys breaking and entering?"

"Shh." Jon pressed his finger to his lips. "Don't tell."

She stepped inside, happy at least that he hadn't wasted a trip while not so happy the locks on her home were such a joke it took him seconds to get in. Flipping on lights, which he hadn't bothered to do, she glanced toward the back of the house. "I'm a little freaked out."

"I'm sorry. I shouldn't have—"

"No, it's not that you got in. More at the thought that anybody else could."

"I understand. You might want to invest in an alarm service. I have one."

"You do?" Big strong SEALs had alarms on their houses? That was news.

"Yup." He dipped his head. "You can never be too careful."

"I guess not." She drew in a breath and let it out slowly. Glancing up, she caught Jon watching the rise and fall of her breasts beneath the sundress.

Maybe he was interested in her after all.

He took a step forward and laid one big hand on her shoulder. She felt the heat of him against her bare skin. That was one way to get her mind off her security. "I'm sorry I freaked you out. This is a safe neighborhood. I really wouldn't worry."

Ali nodded, having trouble coming up with a coherent response while he touched her. "You want to stay for a little while?"

It wasn't a hard question but he hesitated for long enough, she wondered what was going on inside his head.

Finally, he let out a sigh. "Yeah, I do wanna stay, which is why I'm going to go."

"I don't understand." She did however take note his hand had remained on her shoulder. For a man intent on going he hadn't made a move to leave yet.

"I'm afraid if I stay, I won't want to leave."

Ali swallowed hard and leaned just a bit closer to him. "Then don't leave."

She saw his chest rise and fall, watched his focus drop to her lips before he brought it back up to her eyes. "You don't do one-night stands."

"I said I hadn't in the past, not that I was opposed to having one. With you."

"This can't be anything more than tonight."

Pulse racing, Ali nodded. "I know."

His breathing grew more rapid as his eyes narrowed. Taking a step forward, he slid his leg between hers as he cupped her face with his palm. He leaned low, his lips nearing hers when he halted and mouthed a silent curse.

"What's wrong?"

"I don't have any condoms." Jon pulled back.

Reaching out, Ali fisted the fabric of his T-shirt to keep him right where he was. "I do."

"Do you?" Hovering close, he looked as much amused as surprised.

"There was a bridal shower for a girl at work last week. The party favors were condoms."

"I'm very happy to hear that." Smiling, he closed the small distance and Ali anticipated the first taste of his kiss.

CHAPTER FIVE

The man kissed like he seemed to do everything—with enthusiastic perfection.

Ali tried to speculate that it was his strong work ethic combined with an overt alpha male competitive nature that drove Jon to excel. That was better than thinking his skill at kissing had been achieved through years of practice on hundreds of women.

It was easy to believe Jon was a perfectionist. Even today when Darci had not so subtly singled out Ali and Jon to husk the corn for dinner Jon had gone above and beyond, not leaving even one strand of silk on any ear. Then, quick and efficient, he'd cleaned up their work area and dispatched with the garbage, carrying it all the way out to the trash bin. Anyone walking through the kitchen would have never known they'd husked a dozen ears of corn moments before.

She could certainly appreciate a job well done, especially when it entailed a good and thorough kiss. With full body participation on his part, Jon treated Ali to just that. He captured and held her tightly with both hands. One large palm wrapped around her neck to cradle the base of her head, while the other clasped her hip as he pressed close.

A low groan of satisfaction rumbled from within his chest as he tipped his head and breached her lips with his tongue, deepening the kiss. One thigh moved farther between hers, causing a delicious friction in a region she'd too long ignored. Her own sound of satisfaction mimicked his.

Jon drew in a sharp breath in response and pulled back, breaking the kiss. "Bedroom?" He asked the one-word question from just inches away from her face.

She could see his blue eyes narrowed with need. Could feel the warmth of his breath brush her lips.

Swallowing hard, Ali managed a small nod. Lightheaded, she felt as if she had to try to remember to breathe or she'd pass out. Of course if she did, Jon was big and strong enough to pick her up and carry her to the bedroom.

Deep in her Scarlett and Rhett fantasy, she had to work to not be disappointed when Jon grabbed her hand instead of sweeping her into his arms. He glanced expectantly at the selection of doors and she realized he didn't know which one led to the bedroom.

Good thing she'd lived there for a few years or she might have had trouble remembering where the room was herself. Taking a man she'd just met to bed was proving nerve wracking. Or maybe it was just the sex hormones flooding her bloodstream that made her woozy.

Feeling awkward, she led him by the hand to her bedroom. It would have definitely been easier if he'd swooped her up in his arms, tossed her onto the bed, and ravished her. Ali hated having to take the lead.

Thank goodness once they were actually in the room and she'd flipped on the light switch he took over, stepping close again. Towering over her, he gazed down at his hand as he pushed the straps of both her sundress and bra over the crest of her shoulder. He trailed one fingertip over her heated skin.

"You got some sun today. You should have been wearing sunscreen." Bending low, he moved his mouth over the path his finger had taken.

That stole the reply she'd been about to make about how she had put on sunscreen before she'd left the house but it had been a long day out in the sun.

That's what she would have told him, if she could have gotten her brain to function. He continued slowly exposing her, pushing the neckline of the dress as well as the cup of her bra lower until the heat of his mouth covered the peak of her breast.

Tipping her head back, Ali let her eyelids drift shut as a shudder ran through her. She felt the bulge of his muscles beneath her hands as she grasped onto his biceps, partly because she couldn't stand not touching him and partly because she was feeling a little unsteady and needed something to hold on to.

Electric shocks of pleasure zinged through her as he worked her nipple with his mouth. His hands didn't remain idle. True to form, the man was an overachiever. He traversed the rest of her body with big flat palms that seemed made to cradle her curves. He moved to cup the swell of her behind.

Cool air struck her flesh as he bunched the fabric of her dress and her lacey boy short-cut panties—a skimpy indulgence compared to the practical cotton underwear she usually bought—were exposed.

Ali had spent most of her adult life being dissatisfied with her body. Even so, she'd happily be naked with this man, pressed skin to skin. His hard-bodied, SEAL-worthy physical excellence should have been intimidating. Instead it only made her want to rub against him like a cat would. She might even purr, if given the chance.

He pushed the hem of her dress higher until he settled his hands at her waist and she realized that fantasy had a very good chance of becoming reality and soon.

Holding the dress out of the way with his left hand, his right hand moved around to her belly. She tightened her muscles, holding her stomach in and trying to make it as flat as possible, but he didn't remain there. As he moved to tease her neck with his mouth, he snaked his hand down and beneath the top band of her underwear, then down farther.

She drew in a sharp breath as his fingers reached their goal and pressed against the nerve endings that craved attention. Her reaction made him smile. She felt it against her throat before he moved up her neck toward her ear. That, in combination with the motion of his fingers teasing her closer to orgasm, was beginning to make her weak in the knees.

Much more of this and she'd fall right off her new cork wedge-heeled sandals. As if sensing her unsteadiness, Jon supported her with one splayed palm flat against her back. With his hand braced low, near the base of her spine, he held her firm and close—not that she had any intention of going anywhere. Not with what was going to be one hell of a climax hovering just out of reach.

Her breath came faster, in gasps tinged with tiny sounds she couldn't control. When he drew her earlobe between his teeth and groaned, the orgasm broke, sending waves of pleasure pulsing through her. The heat of his mouth against her ear pushed her to another level of need. One that would only be satisfied by having him completely.

When she could breathe again, she said, "Bed."

Jon's gaze shot toward the bed and he let out a short breathy laugh as he pulled his hand out of her underwear. "My thoughts exactly. Those condoms nearby?"

Still not standing all that steady, Ali maintained her grip on his arms. He didn't seem to mind. She sure as hell didn't. "In the nightstand drawer."

"Mmm. Perfect." He glanced down at her dress. "I want you naked."

The words sent her heart fluttering. "Okay. You too."

"Not a problem." He grinned as he tugged his shirt over his head and tossed it onto the dresser. As

Ali feasted on the view of the bare chest she'd fantasized about for most of the day, Jon reached for his belt. "Memories of tonight are going to have to last me a very long time. I'm not letting anything get in my way."

The intensity of that promise had her hands shaking as she reached behind her to unzip the dress. Jon paused in unbuttoning his shorts to turn her around.

Her back to him, Ali felt the mass of his body behind her, the motion of his big capable hands maneuvering the tiny tab of the zipper slowly down, loosening the fabric until it fell away from her body.

It all combined to twist her overwhelming need to have him. All of him.

Her dress hit the floor with a soft rustle and she stood before him in nothing but her good lace underwear and her not so nice everyday-wear bra. She could only hope he was too distracted to notice that small detail. She also vowed to go shopping immediately for nicer undergarments now that it seemed she was indeed the one-night stand type.

His touch set her on fire as he unhooked her bra clasp. She sloughed off the offending bra as he ran his rough palms down her sides to settle on her hips. He leaned low and nuzzled her neck while the heat of the skin of his chest pressed against her back.

These were the kind of things dreams were made of. Ali realized there was no way she was going to let herself feel bad about giving in to her desire for this man. Maybe she'd feel the full weight of her decision tomorrow or the next day, or in a week or a month after he'd deployed, but not now.

"Get on the bed." His words, spoken low and close to her ear, set her heart racing at a new level. Jon dropped his hold on her. She missed his touch—both steadying and unnerving at the same time—but turned to watch him finish getting undressed.

Blindly, she moved toward the bed, her eyes on him the entire time as he kicked off his deck shoes and pushed his shorts down his thick thighs. Then his boxer briefs followed and the erection that she'd seen outlined by the cotton before was bared to view.

Ali crashed into the edge of the bed. She reached out to catch herself, landing on her hands rather than her face, which made the clumsy move slightly less embarrassing. With such a distraction in the room, it was no wonder she couldn't even manage to walk. She pushed up to right herself, but he was behind her in a flash.

"No. Stay just like this." He prompted her to stay in her current position with the touch of one hand against her back.

Standing while she bent over the edge of the mattress, Jon hooked his fingers beneath her underwear and tugged them all the way down her legs.

When they were around her high platform heels, she stepped out of them, noting he made no move to take her sandals off. He did however take advantage of her position by bending low and laving her entrance with his tongue, plunging it inside her channel.

She was happy she was leaning on the mattress

as his tongue moved to tease her more and more and her knees weakened.

Then, he pulled away. "This drawer here?"

Ali swallowed as he asked about the condoms and the reality of this crazy encounter felt even more real. Still, she answered, "Yes."

The fact the rubbers were colored and fruit-flavored and had cutesy little stickers with the bride and groom's names on them seemed extra ridiculous in her current situation, but he didn't comment. He suited up fast and was back behind her, hands braced on her hips in what seemed like seconds.

Then what she'd been imagining—his plunging inside her—was no longer just in her imagination. She heard his hissed intake of breath as he pushed deep. He held there for a moment, not moving, possibly not breathing, before he set a steady rhythm.

When she'd been expecting for him to let loose, had expected him to move hard and fast, he did the opposite. Jon moved slow and steady, taking her thoroughly and with intent. She'd never been a huge fan of this particular position, but she had to begin to reevaluate that opinion. Jon seemed to hit just the right spot with every downward stroke, before pulling back in an agonizingly slow dance that sent tingles up her spine.

She didn't want to interfere with his cadence but soon found herself rocking back against him. The result was his motion speeding, but Ali had nothing to complain about as the sensations rocketing through her increased.

They were coming closer to the crescendo with every stroke, but she didn't want it to end.

With every fiber of her being she knew he would get dressed and leave her the moment he was finished. Instinct told her Jon was not the kind of man who snuggled and spooned after sex. She wished he were.

Breathing hard, he pushed in deep and held and she waited for it to end, but it didn't. Jon wrapped his arms around her and then reached low. One press of his finger on just the right spot had her hips tipping forward to push harder against his touch.

Leaning against her back, he laid his cheek against her hair. "Come with me."

"I don't know if I—"

"Try."

Something about him made her want to please him, to do exactly as he asked, and the way he worked her with his hand while gently rocking inside her made it easy to comply. She gyrated in time with his motion as her muscles bore down and the feeling of impending release built inside her.

As her mouth opened so she could draw deeper breaths, he groaned behind her. "Yes."

The intensity of that single word spoken close pushed her over the edge. He pumped hard and fast and followed right after. They came together with her clasped tightly in his arms.

He stayed like that, his weight crushing her into the mattress, them both fighting to recover their breath. She didn't know how long the moment lasted. Not long enough was the only thing she was sure of when he untangled his arms, braced against the mattress and pushed off her.

Ali lifted her head in time to see him pad, naked and gorgeous, across the carpeted floor toward the bathroom door. She'd expected to see his hot tight little butt cheeks, and she wasn't at all surprised by the wide expanse of his back muscles that narrowed to his waist. What was a shock was the tattooed set of angel wings that covered the skin from his shoulders nearly all the way down to the dimples on his lower back.

She wanted to ask him about them. Wanted to trace the ink with her finger as he stretched out nude next to her in bed. Craved him over her, inside her, while she raked her nails down his back. Instead, she decided to cover up her own nakedness.

What to put on was the question. Not her clothes from that day. It was late enough she could put on her pajamas, but that might look as if she assumed he would crawl into bed with her for the night, which she had a feeling could force him out the door even more quickly.

Deciding that a T-shirt and the shorts made out of sweatpants material that she wore on the treadmill would look comfortable and casual without setting any expectations, she yanked open drawers and pulled the items on. One glance in the mirror told her that her hair was a mess. She tugged at the elastic band holding it up and it tumbled to her shoulders. She fluffed it as best she could, turning just as Jon emerged from the bathroom.

For a loss at what to talk about after what she'd just done with a man she didn't know all that much about, she said, "Nice tattoo."

"Thanks." A crooked grin tipped up the corner of his mouth. "Just don't let it fool you. I'm no angel."

"I wouldn't assume that for a moment." She forced a smile as she stood awkwardly next to the dresser while he bent to retrieve his underwear.

When he reached for his shorts next, she was pretty sure he was leaving. They'd already gotten what they'd both wanted. She had work in the morning. He probably had some SEAL duties early too. Why would he stay?

All of those good reasons still didn't make her wish he would stay any less, proving she wasn't wired to do one-night stands. She was an all-or-nothing kind of gal. Given Jon's profession and imminent deployment it was clear that if those were the only two choices she was going to end up with nothing.

But like he'd said, at least they had the memories. His to keep him occupied during what she assumed would be a long sexless deployment. Hers to console herself with during her own lonely nights.

While she'd pondered the situation, he'd finished getting dressed. He glanced her direction as he slid the end of his belt through the buckle. "Walk me to the door?"

With her heart pounding harder at the thought of saying goodbye than it had before their sexual encounter, Ali forced herself to sound casual as she said, "Sure."

He led the way back to the front door, glancing at the back of the house along the way. "About that back entrance. . . If you go to the hardware store and pick up a chain, you can install it pretty easily yourself. Or call Rick. I'm sure he'd help you."

This was the kind of talk she could get from the guy working at the hardware store. It wasn't what she wanted during the last moments she would spend with the man who'd just been inside her.

Though it was sweet that he was concerned for her safety. "Okay. Thanks."

Jon turned to face her fully. "I'm going to be gone very soon and for a long time."

She read between the lines. He was telling her not to expect a post-coital phone call before he left. "I know."

"It's fighting season over there. I can't afford to be distracted."

And now he was saying, in his roundabout way, for her not to expect an email or letter while he was gone either. "I understand."

"And even when I'm home, the schedule, the hours, the demands are insane. It's the kind of shit that breaks up marriages."

Jeez. She got it. Most men would probably just say goodbye and disappear. She didn't know if she respected him more or less after this run of preemptive excuses.

"Jon, I knew what I was getting into when I invited you in." She managed a smile and tried to lighten the mood with a joke. "I mean, before you broke in."

He didn't laugh, but instead shook his head. He surprised her when he reached up and cupped her face with both palms. His gaze was intense as it met and held hers. "I'm screwing this up badly. What

I'm trying to say is, Ali, you're the kind of woman who could easily be a distraction if I let you."

That wasn't what she'd expected. She managed to say, "Oh."

"If I want to come home alive, I can't let you." His words as much as his touch sent a flood of warmth through her heart, just when she should be locking that organ down tight before it got broken by this man who was telling her he was going away and she'd never hear from him again.

His lips covered hers before she was forced to come up with a response she didn't have, and she was relieved.

Getting lost in his kiss was too easy considering this was goodbye forever. She tried to memorize every nuance of this last moment they'd have together. The feel of his hands on her. The intensity of his tongue plunging against hers. Even the rough scrape of his stubble against the skin surrounding her lips.

He was hard again. She felt it pressing against her. It was all she could do to stop herself from reaching for him. From unzipping those shorts.

To hell with it. If this was to be the last time she saw him, she wasn't going to deny herself anything. Ali reached between them and stroked his length through his shorts. A groan rumbled through him.

Encouraged, she eased the zipper down. Her hand was small enough she could slip it through the opening. He stiffened as she maneuvered his erection free of his underwear and out through the open fly, all without taking his shorts off.

With the full hard length of him exposed, she

went down onto her knees. Glancing up, she saw him watching her as she slid him between her lips. His nostrils flared as his eyes narrowed but never left her face.

After his goodbye speech, she half expected him to stop her. He didn't. Instead, he slid his fingers through her hair. His hands remained on her, bracing her head as he stroked in and out of her mouth.

Nope, he definitely wasn't fighting this and she was happy to provide one more memory. Maybe this would make it a little bit harder, make him regret it a tad bit more, as he worked to force her out of his mind.

Ali wanted to be his biggest distraction—sad but true given what he'd said about having to block out everything if he wanted to come home alive.

To up the ante even more, she locked her gaze on his, not breaking contact as he plunged so deep she felt him in the back of her throat and had to fight her gag reflex. She was determined to be unforgettable, and he wasn't arguing with her.

A frown creased his brow. His chest rose and fell as his breathing sped. She added a hand to the mix, working him double time. She tasted the prelude to his orgasm before he held her head and thrust deep. With a loud groan, he emptied himself into the back of her throat.

She felt the shudder run through him as the throbbing slowed to a stop. He pulled out of her mouth. "I'm sorry."

"For what?" She stood.

"I had no intention of letting that go so far."

"I had no intention of stopping until it did."

He laughed and shook his head. "You're making it hard to leave, you know."

That was her plan. Ali cocked a brow. "Am I? Sorry." She wasn't sorry one little bit.

Jon drew in a breath and backed her against the door. He dropped his forehead to hers. "I had a good day. Not just this part, but all of it."

"Me too. Even shucking the corn."

"Yeah, even that." A smile bowed his lips before it disappeared as he said, "I'm going to go now."

"Okay." She noticed he wasn't moving yet. After another intake of breath, he kissed her forehead and pushed away. She moved so he could reach the doorknob and open the door.

Standing in the opening, he glanced back at her. She waited for him to say something. *Good-bye. Thanks for the blow job.* Something. Anything. Instead he tipped his head in a small nod, stepped outside and pulled the door closed behind him.

That was it then. In less than an hour this man had captured her heart, loved her and then left her.

It had to be the quickest beginning, middle and ending to a romance in the history of the world.

CHAPTER SIX

Ali's phone rang not two minutes after the door had closed behind Jon. The read-out said *Darci*. She grabbed it and hit to answer, not bothering with hello. "Are you stalking me?"

"No, why?" Darci sounded confused.

"Nothing." Ali dismissed her delusion that Darci could have known that Jon had just left. "What's going on?"

"I just wanted to make sure you got home safe."

Bullshit. "No, you wanted to see if he was still here."

"Um, maybe. So is he?" Darci sounded absolutely bubbly over the possibility.

"Sorry to disappoint you, but no." No one was more disappointed about that fact than Ali herself.

"Bummer. Did you at least get to talk a bit?"

Before she could stop it, a burst of a bitter laugh that would tell Darci more than Ali was willing to let out shot from between her lips. "Yeah, we talked."

"All right, something happened. I know you too well so don't try to lie. Tell me."

Darci was right. They did know each other too well. Besides that, Ali was a crappy liar. "Well, I took your advice."

"What advice?"

"To have a fling."

"What?" Her friend's voice rose a good octave higher than usual.

"Yup. We had sex." More than once. Well, actually one and a half times if she counted the parting blow job on the floor by the front door. Jeez, what the hell had gotten into her? "Remember, you promised not to judge."

"I'm not judging. I'm just surprised. And what the hell? How are you done and he's gone already? Oh my God." The volume of Darci's voice dropped low. "Is Jon one of those quick-on-the-trigger guys?"

She laughed. "No. He's one of those get-out-quick-afterward kind of guys."

"Aw, Ali. I'm so sorry. I never thought—"

"No, it's okay. Don't be sorry. It's not your fault. I knew what it was going in. He's leaving the country. We discussed it and agreed that this was just a one-time thing. No communications. No repeats." God, laying it out for Darci made Ali feel even worse about the whole thing.

"What a bastard. No communications, my ass. He knows very well that they have email over there. Hell, they can even call on the phone or get on video chat. I had no idea he was such an ass—"

"No, really. It wasn't like that. We both agreed this was best." And now Ali was defending him, when actually, she'd like to agree with Darci.

Yes, Ali had agreed to a one-night stand because he was deploying, but saying she could do it didn't mean she actually believed that's what tonight would be. Somewhere in the back of her brain where the little girl who believed in fairy tales and happy endings still lived, she'd hoped it would turn out to be more.

"It's still shitty of him to run out the door, in my opinion. He could have at least stayed the night."

Didn't she know it. "It's better this way. I have to work tomorrow and I'm tired. I think all the sun got to me so I'm going to head to bed. I'll see you in the morning?"

"Okay. And Ali?"

"Yeah?"

"I'm sorry I pushed you at Jon."

Her too. Ali drew in a breath and let it out in a sigh. "Goodnight."

~ * ~

Jon's phone buzzed in the pocket of his uniform pants. He knew it wasn't command calling him in because that summons had already come, hence the reason he was driving to base at twenty-one hundred on a holiday.

The colored burst of Fourth of July fireworks from somewhere in the distance rising above the trees caught his attention as he steered with one hand and reached into his pocket for the phone with the other.

Rick's name was on the display. He punched the button to answer. "Dude. What's up?"

"Good question. That's what I wanted to ask you."

How could Rick know the team had been recalled to deploy tonight? He was supposed to be out of the loop. Christ, operational security was becoming an absolute joke.

Frowning, Jon asked, "How did you know?"

"I overheard Darci on the phone with Ali. I asked her what was going on and she told me."

What the hell?

"Wait, what?" Unless Ali was some super spy who'd planted a bug on him, or a crazy stalker who'd followed him, it was impossible he and Rick were talking about the same thing. "What are you talking about?"

"You had sex with Ali and then left like your hair was on fire."

And this was why even with as much as he liked it, he usually didn't have sex—all the crap that went along with it. "Is that what Ali said?"

"No, I don't think she used those exact words." Rick was hedging, like he'd supplied his own words and not Ali's. That made Jon feel moderately better.

"Then what were her exact words?"

"I don't know. I didn't talk to her. All I know is that Darci called Ali not long after you two left here, and she said you'd already left, which in my mind didn't leave a whole lot of time in the middle."

Jon shook his head as he began to wonder how much this story had changed as it passed from Ali, to Darci, to Rick and now to him.

"Listen, not that it's any of your business, but I didn't rush out." Jon just hadn't stayed around for very long after. As it turns out, it was a good thing he hadn't. He'd just gotten home when he'd gotten called in.

As he neared the gate and the sign reading *No Handheld Cell Phones* came into view, he said, "Hang on, Rick. I have to put the phone down."

He rolled down his window and slowed to a stop, flashing his ID to the guard.

The guard greeted him, and then waved him through. When Jon had rolled the window back up and hit the button to put the cell on speakerphone, he heard only silence.

"Rick? You still there or did I lose you?"

After a second's hesitation, Rick said, "I'm here. You're on base."

No use lying about it. "Yeah, I am."

Another pause told Jon that Rick knew why. The most likely reason for the command to pull Jon in at this hour, just days before deployment, was because the unit was leaving earlier than scheduled.

"All right." Rick drew in a breath before he continued. "You got a message you want me to deliver?"

"No. Rick, Ali and I talked. We're good. She agreed with me on everything. It's crazy to keep in touch. It is what it is."

"Okay. I'll stay out of your business." Rick agreed, but beneath his words Jon heard the sadness.

The unit had been on missions and trainings

since Rick had left, but this would be their first extended deployment without him. No doubt he was waxing nostalgic, maybe even wishing that he were shipping out with his old teammates.

"You? Stay out of my business? Doubtful." Jon made a joke to try and lighten the heavy mood.

"Yeah, well, deal with it." There was a pause before Rick added, "Stay safe, brother."

"That's the plan. I'll touch base with you when I can."

"I'd appreciate that. Night."

"Night." Jon disconnected. As he pulled into a parking space, he tried to wrestle his mind back to where it needed to be. Not on Ali or Rick, but rather on all he'd have to do.

There'd be no sleep for the weary tonight.

CHAPTER SEVEN

They didn't speak. There was no need. Countless hours of training and hundreds of missions with these same men meant they worked together like a well-oiled machine.

Nothing more than shadows on the cold moonless night, the team moved into place without a sound. They were ready for this. They had rehearsed almost this exact close-quarters battle scenario in the kill house countless times stateside. They'd reviewed it verbally a dozen times this week alone, so that now muscle memory and conscious thought melded seamlessly.

One nod from Zane, a green ghost through the tubes of the night vision goggles, told Jon all he needed to know. They were ready to move.

Zane took point and headed for the point of entry first. Jon followed closely behind him, his breath forming condensation in the December air.

They kept to the sides of the doorway in case the occupants had gotten wise to this little surprise visit and decided to spray the door with automatic gunfire in hopes of hitting whoever was standing on the other side.

Crouched low, Zane reached up with one gloved hand and tried the knob.

It seemed crazy, but more times than not the doors of their targets were unlocked, providing the team an open path and the element of surprise.

During Jon's first mission as a SEAL, they'd patrolled in at night, silently on foot, right up to a suspected insurgent hideout in Afghanistan. He'd waltzed through the unlocked front door and right up to the sleeping fighters.

Even though he had been only renting an apartment at the time, Jon had installed a deadbolt on his front door and a lock on his bedroom the day after returning home to the States.

Not that he was planning on someone sneaking in and shooting him in the night just miles from his base in Virginia, but shit happened. If word got out about what he did for a living, some radical faction could decide to make an example of him or retaliate for one of the many missions he'd been on over the years. As far as terrorists went, the decapitated head of a Navy SEAL was the most coveted trophy of all.

Call him chicken, but Jon would be damned if anyone would be able to accuse him of not learning from other people's stupid mistakes, so he locked down his home tight and slept more soundly for it each night.

Zane glanced at Jon and shook his head.

Unfortunately, tonight's target had learned the same lesson. This particular door was locked. It looked to be a thick one too with a heavy metal handle.

Jon motioned to the sledgehammer sticking out of the pack on his back. They could knock the handle off the door and burst in. Zane shook his head once and pointed to a breaching charge, the long strip of adhesive explosive they both carried in the front of their vests.

Their sneak attack would be exposed either way they chose, but at least blowing the door was a more sure method. He'd run across doorknobs heavy enough to bounce the sledge right off without having any impact on the mechanism.

With any luck, the inhabitants would be so disoriented from the blast it would buy the team a few precious seconds and they would retain the upper hand.

Still crouched low, Zane adhered the explosive strip to the door.

"Going explosive." Zane's low voice came over the COMM, funneled directly into Jon's right ear. The communication went to the rest of the squad as well—one posted as guard making sure no one snuck up on the unit, and two more covering the back of the house.

Jon rolled to the side along the wall to shield his face from any flying shrapnel as Zane did the same on the other side. The flash and boom was their signal to go, and both men moved at once.

Zane kicked in the door. No longer held shut by the mangled hardware, it opened wide with not much resistance. He went toward the left and swept his weapon in an arc. Jon, close behind, moved toward the right, mirroring Zane's movements.

As he cleared into the room, Jon heard the sound of suppressed fire outside. The bad guys didn't generally bother with suppressors on their weapons, which meant his guys were shooting. Jon had his own task to complete before he could wonder about what was happening behind the dwelling.

The main room right inside the door of the house appeared empty. At least, empty of people. He couldn't say the same about the crap crowding the tight space. It looked like a television episode of *Hoarders*. Besides the stove, table and multiple chairs that filled the room, there were stacks upon stacks of shit. Boxes. Prayer rugs. Garbage.

Busting into a room and not knowing what was inside was bad enough, but not being able to see more than fifty percent of the space because of all the junk made it so much worse. Jon had to physically check behind piles before he felt confident enough to believe the front room was clear.

With a glance in Jon's direction, Zane moved to the closed door in the back wall, the only other door in the room.

It had to lead to a bedroom, and between the gunfire out back and them blowing the front door, whoever was inside that room had to know they were there.

Jon dipped his head to indicate he was ready. As point man, Zane stood off to the side of the doorframe and reached for the knob. It turned in his hand. He shoved the door wide and began shouting to the occupants in Pashto with a few English words thrown in.

Two men sat on the floor on bedrolls, legs crossed, hands behind their heads. They knew, because word had spread like wildfire, that if the Americans didn't see a weapon in a suspect's hand or within reach, they couldn't shoot. The most Jon's team could do was detain the men. Even known insurgents—fighters who they knew had killed Americans—could only be held for a short time for questioning if they didn't have a weapon.

The team would search the house and, if they found anything, bring the men in. They'd be questioned and then released within days, most likely to be picked up again next month after they'd had plenty of time to transport more weapons, gather more followers, shoot at more peacekeepers. Then, orders would come down for another raid. Another opportunity for Jon's squad to put their lives on the line for what amounted to nothing.

And so the grueling cycle would repeat.

Being part of historic events like taking out Osama Bin Laden was rare. Not every mission could be sexy and Jon was fine with that, but it was hard to stay motivated when the results of their missions were so clearly ineffective.

Years ago when Jon had signed up for this life knowing all the sacrifices he'd be making, things had been different. When faced with an apparent threat, they could eliminate that threat without fear of disciplinary action. Slowly, Washington D.C. politics and the media's opinion had trumped everything else, including his safety, causing changes in training, procedure and for Jon, the very essence of the job.

There was an old guy who hung around at the bar back home. He'd been a New York City cop for years until, after putting in his twenty, he'd retired and moved south. A few drinks and all the guy could do was bitch. Complain about how he'd arrest a criminal only to see him out on the same street corner a week later, until finally he started to not give a shit. Eventually, he hadn't even bothered arresting them. Instead he took to waving at them as he sat in the squad car and drank his coffee.

During this deployment—Jon's first rotation in the region since more changes had been implemented to further good relations with the locals as the Joint Forces moved toward turning control of the country over to the Afghan government and military—Jon knew exactly how that old cop had felt—ineffective.

"Two males of fighting age. No visible weapons," Jon reported what he and Zane had found into the COMM for the rest of the team. He remembered hearing the shots outside and asked, "What have you got?"

"Single male fighting age, armed with an AK and grenades." The report came back in Grant's voice. "He must have been on guard duty. He was taking a leak when he spotted us moving in. Swung his weapon at us. We engaged."

And neutralized the threat so they had one less to worry about. Jon nodded. "Copy. Securing detainees now."

"Copy. Beginning search of the property," Grant

responded.

After finding only two unarmed men in the house, Jon suspected that the chances of any significant cache of weapons being nearby would be slim. The arms and explosives would likely be hidden farther away. If they found them in the short time allotted for the unit to stay safely on site and search, they would photograph the evidence and then blow it up to make sure it didn't stay operational to be used to kill again. They were still allowed to do that—at least until the headquarters staff got the bright idea they should start toting the shit back down the mountain while wearing sixty pounds of gear. God preserve them all from the head shed's *good ideas*.

After securing the two men with zip cuffs, Zane turned toward Jon. "This was supposed to be a stronghold and they've got one guard outside and these two inside, unarmed and sleeping. Where are all the weapons? Where are the supposed recruits being trained?"

Jon had no doubt they'd find some weapons, eventually, after they'd searched through the crap inside the dwelling, but Zane was right. Something was off. The promised payload didn't seem to be there.

It had been there five days ago. The squad had seen the satellite images captured by the drone. There'd been lots of activity. Many men carrying boxes in and out of the building.

"My bet is it was here, but it got moved while we sat around waiting for orders to come down."

"Six hour hike up a goat trail for nothing." Zane

shook his head.

Jon let out a snort. "At least the way back is downhill."

They were supposedly the best of the best, and they'd just been sent on what amounted to a wild goose chase.

"Yeah, downhill while dragging these two with us," Zane pointed out.

Yes, that would make the long, cold trek more challenging, and they wanted to be back inside the wire before sunrise, which meant they had to hurry.

With the men facedown in the corner of the room with their hands bound behind them, Zane started to paw through the bedding. "There's nothing here. I'm fucking tired of this shit."

"You and me both, buddy. Just remember, one more month and then we're out of here."

Back home to Virginia. There his unit would train hard, usually three out of four weeks a month when they weren't called out on missions, all in preparation to deploy again a few months down the road. In past, Jon had looked forward to the change. The days split between PT, time on the shooting range, and in the kill house for close-quarters battle training. But after so many years, it didn't feel like much of a change anymore.

Something had to give, he only hoped it wasn't him.

~ * ~

A fifteen-minute encounter with the insurgents—which included searching the premises for Intel to bring back and destroying weapons on site—amounted to two hours worth of paperwork back on base. The modern military was choking on its own red tape and not even those in the Naval Special Warfare Development Group were exempt from it.

Even though he was done with the paperwork, Jon's workday—which happened at night since his unit worked vampire hours—wasn't finished yet. As the early morning sun rose higher over the horizon, he and the unit had to sit through a meeting as well.

He did his best to focus on his commander's words as he sat in the chair that was beginning to feel much too comfortable.

"The command thinks it would be a good idea—"

Every man in the room let out a low groan at the commander's words, Jon included.

That was another thing that was bound to kill the military, or at least a few of its men—the *good idea fairy*. Jon had survived the raid. He'd survived the trip back down the mountain. He'd survived the masses of paperwork, but as he sat in the war room and listened to the commander, he realized he might not survive the good idea fairy.

The commander's only reaction was to paste on a scowl and continue, "—if we announced ourselves before entering the building."

Zane raised one hand. "Announced ourselves how?"

"Like the police do. A statement of whom we are followed by instructions for anyone inside to put down their weapons and come out with their hands behind their head."

The silence felt ripe with the many unspoken

comments on the latest idea, but not a man spoke a word.

The commander's gaze swept the room. "Questions? Comments?"

Besides *what the fuck,* Jon had nothing, though he was sure the opinions would be flying later, once he and the guys were in private. By the expression on the commander's face, he felt the same as the rest of them but like them, his hands were tied.

Command might as well have literally tied all of their hands. That wouldn't have been much different than sending them out there to announce themselves to the bad guys. Maybe they could get them some bull's eye targets to hang on their chests as well, to make it easier for the enemy to kill them.

The commander dismissed them, and the unit moved out of the room. It wasn't until they'd reached their quarters that the grumbling began.

"Announce ourselves?" Zane's eyes widened in disbelief. "Are they kidding?"

Sitting on the edge of his rack to yank off one boot, Thom let out a puff of air. "We might as well forget about the night missions and just walk up to the front door in broad daylight."

"Better yet, let's just drop them a letter. Let 'em know when we're fixin' to come. Then maybe they'll all relocate and we won't have to go at all." Brody shook his head, and then glanced at Jon. "You're awfully quiet. Don't tell me you have no opinion on this bullshit."

Jon had plenty of opinions, but not one would do them any good. He shrugged. "Let's just get out of this shithole and back to the states alive."

His goal was getting home before the good idea fairy made a casualty out of him. After that, he'd have to see. Until then, he'd take it one day at a time. He'd done it before.

Sometimes, when surviving even a single day seemed too overwhelming, it was more like one hour at a time. Jon flashed back to BUD/S, when his future as a SEAL depended on both physical and mental endurance and the instructors made sure to test both beyond the limits. He remembered making deals with himself on a daily basis—*just get through until lunch*. Then, after he accomplished that, he'd think *I just have to make it until dinner*.

Hell Week deprived the candidate of sleep until some men hallucinated, put them in the cold ocean water for so many hours they nearly reached the point of hypothermia, but they always were fed in exchange for their efforts. That they'd get even a short break in the torturous training to eat was the one thing he'd depend on and he'd held on to that knowledge like a life preserver.

Sad that in light of how he was feeling right now, those seemed like the good old days.

Jon forced his mind to brighter things. "I got an email from Rick."

Grant glanced up. "Yeah? What's up with him?"

"He and Darci are having a New Year's Eve party. He says if we're home in time, we're all invited."

Zane let out a snort. "Hope he doesn't expect an RSVP. We'll know when we'll be home about the same time we touch down."

"You ain't kidding." Brody laughed as his gaze

cut sideways to Jon. "So, he's still living with Darci?"

"Seems like." Jon nodded.

Brody nodded but didn't comment, even though Jon had fully expected some razzing about Rick living with his little sister. That had Jon wondering. Was Brody more interested in Rick's current living situation or Darci's? Definitely an intriguing concept since Brody and Darci had always been polite with each other, but that was it. Brody's brother Chris, on the other hand, teased the girl relentlessly, like a schoolboy pulling the pigtails of the girl he liked. Maybe Brody was inquiring on behalf of his brother. Interesting.

Thoughts of Darci brought up memories of Ali, which happened far too often for Jon's liking considering he'd been the one to set the limits between them. One night of fun. No communications afterward.

Even so, when Jon had first arrived in Afghanistan, he'd half expected to find an email from Ali waiting on him. He figured it would be easy enough for her to wrangle his email address out of Rick by way of Darci. Then again, he sensed she was smart so she and Darci could probably figure out his email all by themselves. If Ali inserted his name in lieu of Rick's in his old military email address, she'd come up with Jon's. It wasn't as if the government used a real tough code to create those addresses.

But there'd been no email, or letter, or care package. Crazy as it seemed, he couldn't deny the undercurrent of disappointment he felt that she'd actually stuck to their agreement.

Maybe she *was* pissed at him for running out so fast that night.

The memory of her on her knees by the door, big hazel eyes staring up at him as she deep-throated him, had a long unsatisfied need surfacing from deep within. Over five months later he could relive that night in his mind with such vivid, visceral recollection it made him weak in the knees. Of course, it had been five sexless months spent in a comfortless hellhole, so that could be part of the problem.

Once he was home, Jon figured he'd be able to get his head on straight. But when he thought about getting back to Virginia, he didn't think about hitting the bar his first night and seeing who he could bring home, like Zane probably would.

Jon wasn't going back to his wife like Grant was, or to his kids like Thom. When Jon thought of getting off that bus on base, getting into his truck and heading somewhere for his first night back, he thought of Ali. Pictured driving to her house. Knocking on that front door she'd forgotten her key to. Kissing her silly while backing her up all the way to the bedroom where he'd spend the next eight or so hours taking her every way a man could. . .

And now he was hard as a rock. In the middle of the sleeping quarters while surrounded by the guys.

This wasn't good. He'd had plenty of sex with women over the years, so why was this one different?

It had to be because he'd only had that one night. Usually he'd stick it out for a little while, keeping it casual but monogamous, and then something or another would make him break it off. He'd never had that opportunity with Ali. That time to see the flaws, the insurmountable issues.

Maybe that's exactly what he needed. More time with her so he could get her out of his system.

His dick sure liked that plan. It hardened to the throbbing point.

"I'm hitting the showers." Jon announced it to the room in general.

He and his team worked opposite hours of most of the rest of the camp since their missions often depended upon the cover of darkness, but the post-op bullshit had taken so long it was now mid-morning. He hoped to God the showers were empty this time of day. He needed to relieve this pressure somehow and even with a shower curtain to shield him, he'd prefer privacy while he did it.

CHAPTER EIGHT

The door swung wide and the warm glow of the lights inside flooded the doorstep where Ali stood thinking that she should have remembered to wear gloves.

"Ali, hi." Darci smiled. "Happy New Year!"

"Happy New Year to you too." Ali accepted Darci's greeting and hug with a smile, all while balancing the tray of cookies in one cold hand. "Where should I put dessert?"

"On the counter is great. Thanks." Darci backed away from the door. She eyed the tray covered in clear wrap as Ali walked by. "Mmm, those look really good."

"Thanks." Ali had become quite a baker, thanks to the lack of other distractions in her life—such as a boyfriend.

She'd also put on another five pounds. One of the unsung gifts of the holiday season. Tomorrow,

71

along with the rest of the country making resolutions, she'd go on a diet. Until then, there was no use worrying about it. It was a holiday.

Darci, of course, never seemed to gain weight for any reason. Ali pocketed her envy and took in Darci's slinky black dress and higher-than-high heels. "You look nice."

"Thank you. I figure you can't go wrong with basic black, right?"

Ali raised one brow. "Right."

Not if basic black was also cut low in the front to emphasize what little Darci had there, pushed up to the limit by a bra that was working miracles.

Her best friend was dressed to impress. To impress *who* was the question. Ali intended to find out. "So, who's coming?"

Darci's grin told her the answer. Ali's eyes popped wider. "No."

"Yes." She nodded, grinning wider. "They landed in the States yesterday and they should be back to base in time to get here for tonight."

As her brain swirled with a kaleidoscope of thoughts and emotions, Ali knew she had to say something in response to the news that Darci had dropped like a bomb. All she could manage was, "Wow."

The siblings had been hinting that there was a good chance Rick's former team would be stateside some time around now, but even as a civilian Ali had been friends with Darci long enough to know scheduled troop movements changed often, sometimes delayed by weeks. Maybe that was on purpose, to keep everyone in the dark since theoretically no one should know when or where the units were traveling.

It seemed to Ali a whole lot of people knew, at least general information, if not specifics.

None of that mattered. What did matter—what had Ali's heart suddenly pounding—was that she might be seeing Jon again.

It had been six months, almost to the day. She hadn't heard hide nor hair from him since he'd nodded goodbye to her at the front door on July fourth.

How was she going to act around him? Casual was a given, but should she be aloof and uninterested? Or flirty and fun but without any expectations? It seemed beyond her to be around the man who still affected her as if she'd been with him only yesterday.

Six freaking months. Her body and mind should have moved on. But the dreams she occasionally had featuring one sexy dark-haired man and his soaring angel wings of ink—dreams that had her waking feeling needy—told her another story.

"Drink?" Darci's question dragged Ali away from the turmoil happening in her own head. "We have wine, champagne, beer. Soda, vodka, bourbon and some expensive scotch that smells like rotting dirt that Rick likes."

Ali eyed all the bottles on the counter and the big stainless bowl she'd seen Darci use for salad, which tonight contained ice and assorted white wine, champagne and beer bottles. "Champagne is good. Thanks."

In light of who was coming, Ali would need a

big one, and for Darci to keep 'em coming.

Like a bartender, Darci stood on the other side of the kitchen island behind rows of clean glasses and reached for the open bottle of champagne. "Rick wanted to bring the big red cooler inside, but I told him no. So don't worry, we have plenty of everything on hand. It's just outside on the deck.

"This looks much nicer for a party. And I can help keep an eye out and refill it, if you need."

"Thank you. See? I knew a woman would understand." Darci shook her head. "Men."

Men, indeed. Ali wished she had a man to be exasperated about. Even if he were a brother. *Especially* if he was a brother who came with a posse of hot best friends like Rick did.

Standing on the other side of the island where Darci had the bar set up, Ali glanced across the kitchen at the clock on the microwave. "What time are you expecting. . . everyone else?"

"We told people around seven-thirty. Rick invited a couple of guys from the power plant too, so it wouldn't be a pitifully small party if our surprise guests somehow didn't make it. But last reports looked pretty good they'll be here." Darci grinned.

Ali processed that information. She'd arrived a little early in case Darci and Rick had needed help setting up. It wasn't lost on her she'd yet to offer any help as she noticed one host seemed to be missing. "Where's Rick?"

"Out buying more ice." Darci handed Ali the glass she'd just poured, and grabbed the second. "It's not like we could ask the guys to stop at the store on the way over and get us ice after they only stepped foot on US soil less than twenty-four hours ago."

That comment brought Ali's attention back to the subject of Jon, and her mixed feelings over seeing him. "So it's certain then? They're definitely coming tonight?"

"Yeah, I think so. I heard Rick talking on the phone this morning and it sounded like the guys were boarding a plane up north somewhere to get back here. Unless something happened that they couldn't take off, they should be back by now. The single guys like Zane and Jon, should all be here, but I'm not sure about the guys with families. I'm sure Grant's wife has plans. And Thom might want to go straight to see his kids." Darci shrugged.

Ali tried to process that she would indeed be seeing her one-night stand again. Fresh from deployment. Her heart thundered as she wondered if a second one-night encounter six months after the first still counted as a one-night stand or not.

Would it be for only one night this time? Jon wasn't going to be on his way out of the country like last time. Would he want something more?

Ali knew from being friends with Darci that even when not deployed, Rick had traveled a lot. He said it was for training, but they suspected that sometimes it was for missions. Missions the general public wasn't meant to know about. On those occasions, even close family members were kept in the dark.

That secrecy and uncertainty would make it tough to have a relationship, but some guys in the teams managed to do it. Have wives and kids, even.

Funny how back in July Ali had told Darci she wasn't interested in any relationship with any SEAL, and here she was trying to figure out how to have one with Jon. What a difference one hour of incredible sex could make, especially when blown out of proportion by six months of fantasies about it.

The front door opening startled Ali. She spun to see Rick standing in the doorway. He bent to grab a plastic bag full of ice in each hand, and then shouldered the door closed behind him. "Wasn't easy getting this. The first place I went to was sold out. Frigging insane you can't find ice this time of year. It's not like it's beach weather."

"No, but it is probably the biggest party night of the year." Darci moved forward and took the bags from him. "I'll throw these on the back deck. It's cold enough that they should keep fine."

Rick nodded and walked to where Ali stood. "Hey, girl. You look nice."

"Thanks." She'd gone with basic black herself, but unlike Darci's dress, Ali's covered a bit more skin. Of course, that was because Ali had more skin to cover than Darci did.

Rick dropped a kiss on her cheek and Ali had to think how convenient it would be if she could just have feelings for Rick, or him for her. He was nice and cute, and he had a good-paying civilian job with benefits and a pension plan. But alas, Darci's brother had become like the brother Ali never had, and all three of them were happy with that.

Sad that those last criteria Rick possessed were

right up there with the first in Ali's check list of what made for a good man. She felt like an old woman thinking about pensions and health plans as she got closer to the big three-zero.

The sliding back door slammed closed and Darci came back into the house. "Damn, it's cold out there."

"If you'd put on some clothes and dress like it's almost January, you won't be cold, now would you?" Rick reached for a beer bottle and twisted the cap off while shooting Darci a look.

She wrinkled her nose at him. "Oh, shut up. It's a party and it's nice and warm in here."

It was nice and warm in the house, and when a knock on the door had them all turning Ali realized that if who she suspected was standing on the other side it was about to get a whole lot warmer.

"I'll get it." Rick shot a glance over his shoulder. "Get that scotch ready. If it's the team, we're going to need it."

She saw the direction this night could take and it only twisted her insides with more nerves and need. Jon would be drunk on scotch, sexually deprived from a six-month deployment in the war zone, happy to be home and alive. Ali would be just as sexually deprived and a bit tipsy on champagne herself, with no one to kiss at midnight.

Why didn't Rick just present Jon to her naked on a silver platter? She was already salivating like she was a starving woman and Jon was the only meal in sight.

Bracing herself, she donned a smile and watched as Rick pulled open the door. "Dude. Good to see you back in one piece."

"Takes a lot to kill me. You know that." Rick's bulk blocked the entrance, but there was no mistaking the voice of the man at the door who'd replied.

"Come on in. I got some beer cold and the scotch is ready to be poured." Finally, Rick moved out of the way and Jon was there in view.

"Oh, bro. Let me get something in my stomach before I start on the scotch." Jon held up the six-pack he'd carried in. "I grabbed this at the gas station on the way over. Sorry, it's not much. There were slim pickings."

"Don't be silly. You being here is enough, but thanks." Rick took the six-pack from Jon's hands and swung the door shut.

From the kitchen, Darci called out, "Hey, Jon."

Jon, dressed in jeans and a long-sleeved shirt with no coat, moved farther into the room. "Hi, Darci. Happy New Year."

"To you too. Hot hors d'oeuvres are coming out of the oven now, and a lasagna is going in for later."

"Sounds good." Jon's gaze moved from Darci and Ali saw the exact moment he noticed her standing off to the side. He smiled and set her heart fluttering as he came closer until he was standing right there next to her. "Hey. Fancy meeting you here."

"Hi. Welcome home." It was all Ali could do to respond as her throat clenched.

"Thanks. How have you been?" he asked.

"Good. Good. Thanks." She sipped her champagne for lack of anything else to do with her hands or her mouth.

"Good to hear it." Jon turned toward Rick to accept the beer bottle he'd handed him, and that was it. The moment was gone. Not that it had been much of a moment to begin with.

If this stilted attempt at small talk was how the whole night was going to be, she was going to need a refill. She blew out a breath and caught Darci watching her.

Ali put down her glass and moved around the island, into the kitchen area. "Need help with those hors d'oeuvres?"

Darci eyed her with more interest than the question warranted but finally nodded. "Sure. The platter is on the counter. Let me grab a potholder and get them out of the oven."

Jon and Rick moved out to the deck, presumably to stow in the cooler the six-pack Jon had bought. When Jon's overwhelming presence was out of the room, Ali could think again. The way he made her feel, an evening filled with bits of casual conversation and not much else was probably best for everyone involved.

She turned toward the counter and spotted the platter as Darci opened the oven. "Smells good, whatever you're cooking."

Two more big men arrived. Ali recognized Zane and Thom from the Fourth of July party. Since she hadn't seen them around since, she assumed they too were newly returned from the war zone.

After a quick hello to her and Darci, during which Ali could have sworn Darci hiked her boobs a little higher for Zane's benefit, the guys disappeared out onto the deck with Rick and Jon.

The bell rang one more time and Darci moved toward the door. "Brody. Chris. Happy New Year."

"Happy New Year to you too." Chris handed Darci a bouquet of flowers and a box of chocolates. "For the lady of the house."

"Aw, thank you. That's so sweet."

"They're from my brother too. He helped me pick them out." Grinning, Chris hooked a thumb at his brother.

Brody rolled his eyes. "Yeah, I shopped all day."

Darci laughed. "I'm just happy you're back and safe, Brody."

"Thanks." Brody glanced around. "Where's everybody else at?"

It was a valid question since Ali could see through the front window that the driveway and the curb in front of the house had filled up with vehicles, but by the looks of the house, there were only she and Darci there.

"Out on the back deck. Go on out, if you want. But tell them the hors d'oeuvres are ready and they're getting cold."

"Yes, ma'am. Will do." Chris saluted Darci with a grin. He and Brody headed the way Zane and Thom had disappeared, and Ali started to think the party was going to be outside.

She watched them go and frowned. "Aren't they cold out there?"

Darci glanced at the glass door and shrugged. "They'll be in eventually. Probably catching Rick up on war stories."

"Stories they don't want us to hear."

"Apparently not." Darci adjusted the temperature on the oven, looking unconcerned about the little posse on the deck.

Ali, on the other hand, couldn't seem to let the topic go. "But they can tell Rick and Chris, who are both civilians now?"

"I'm sure they're not spilling any state secrets or anything. It's probably some stupid stuff we wouldn't be interested in anyway."

"Hmm, I guess so." Stupid stories or not, as Ali transferred the hot mini quiches from the baking tray to the platter she was feeling left out.

Frustrated—in so many ways—she popped one of the quiches into her mouth. The diet started tomorrow, not tonight.

CHAPTER NINE

"No. You're kidding, right?" Rick shook his head as he glanced around the men circling him on the back deck, the cooler full of beer and bags of ice conveniently at their feet. "I don't believe it."

"Swear to God, dude." Zane held his hand up like he was taking an oath.

Jon nodded. "Yup. It's no lie. We're supposed to stand outside the door, announce who we are and ask them to put down their weapons and come out with their hands behind their heads."

"Wait. So are you supposed to be saying this in Pashto or English?" Rick asked.

"Pfft. Both." Brody let out a snort. "The brass wanna make sure they understand."

"As if we're not giving them enough warning." Thom let out a short laugh. "By the time we tell them in both English and our half-assed Pashto translation, we'll give them plenty of time to get ready to kill us."

"You know, because why shouldn't we give the fighters inside time to mow us down through the door?" Zane shook his head and took a deep pull on his bottle of beer.

"So what are you doing? You're not really following this shit order, are you?"

Zane screwed up his face at Rick's question. "Fuck, no."

Chris smiled. "Better to beg for forgiveness than ask for permission."

Brody blew out a loud breath. "Ain't no asking for forgiveness or anything else from the grave."

"Now guys. You know we're following orders. We've just modified it a bit." And Jon felt perfectly fine with that.

"Yup." Zane nodded. "Now after we blow the door, we shout something close enough to what we're supposed to say as we're going in."

Chris grinned. "That way y'all can swear that you said it."

"Damn right. I'll swear on my momma's grave if I have to." Brody shrugged. "I mean, why not? It ain't a lie."

"Hey, it's printed right on the SEAL website for all to see. *Demand discipline, expect innovation.* We're just innovating." Grinning, Thom shrugged.

Rick shook his head. "Jesus, things have changed."

Chris let out a burst of air. "You ain't hardly kidding."

"Feeling a little better about getting out now?" Jon asked Rick.

"Yeah. Surprisingly. After hearing this shit I am."

"The good idea fairy is only half of it, man." Thom shook his head. "They're so afraid to make any decisions or take any action that we spend half of our time now suited up on standby, waiting for orders."

Zane nodded. "Seriously. They had us ready and on standby for one mission for five damn days."

Rick let out a slow whistle. "Damn."

Chris shook his head. "Makes a man grateful to be a civilian again. And speaking of the advantages of being a civilian, your sister said there's hot food inside. I don't know about y'all but I'm fixin' to get me some."

"Yeah. We should go on in." Rick glanced around the group. "I've kept you out here talking when there's scotch waiting inside."

"The scotch is inside and we're out here?" Chris leveled a gaze at Rick. "Now that right there is a sin."

Jon followed the group inside. Food and scotch sounded pretty damn good. He cleared the sliding glass door and spotted Ali right away. She shot him a glance before turning to do something on the counter, which gave him a nice view of her curves. He remembered the feel of those hips beneath his hands and smiled, appreciating the benefits of being home more and more.

As the other guys moved toward the food, Rick paused next to Jon. "So I didn't get to ask you before the other guys came outside, but have you and Ali talked?"

"Sure. We had a lovely conversation when I arrived."

Rick shook his head. "You know what I meant. Did you talk while you were over there?"

"Not that it's any of your business, but no, we didn't. I told you we agreed before I left that we wouldn't keep in touch. You know that's an impossible situation."

"You're back now."

"I am." Jon had a feeling he knew the reason for Rick stating the obvious.

"So are you gonna start things up again?"

Jon swiveled his head to gawk at Rick. "When exactly did you become so interested in my personal life?"

"When I turned in my separation package and was no longer involved in your military life. Wait and see. It'll happen to you too, when you retire. *If* you don't get shot while announcing yourself to the bad guys first."

"Real nice. Thanks." Jon couldn't help but laugh.

The razzing was all in good fun. You couldn't go through the kind of shit he had with these guys and not be as close as blood brothers. Even so, he wasn't quite ready to admit to Rick that seeing Ali again had put ideas into his head. Imaginings that might possibly become reality if she were willing.

Jon watched her in the kitchen with Darci, both girls laughing at something Chris had said.

Would she be willing? He had to wonder. He couldn't offer her anything more than he had before. A night of fun. Maybe a couple of nights if he saw she was okay with keeping things casual.

Very casual, because there was no place in his life right now for anything more than that.

Rick cracking open the bottle of scotch caught Jon's attention. He guessed it was time to drink, and not just the beer in his hand.

As Rick splashed a long shot into each short glass, Jon eyed the sofa and the reclining chair in the room. "I hope you're planning on a few overnight guests."

Chris came around the island and grabbed a glass. "What are y'all lightweights now?"

"No, but we haven't had anything stronger than the milk that turned sour in the chow hall for six months," Jon reminded him.

"And it's New Year's Eve. Every cop on the force is patrolling for drunk drivers," Thom added.

"Relax. Everyone is welcome to stay the night. There's plenty of room. There's a queen bed in my room and lot's of floor space and I've got a couple of blowup air mattresses in the garage if we need them."

Jon snorted, thinking they'd slept some places so shitty they'd make sleeping on Rick's living room carpet seem like deluxe accommodations at the Ritz.

"I'll just crash with Darci in her room if there's a shortage of space." Chris winked at Darci.

Smiling, she shook her head. "Always the joker."

Jon raised a brow, wondering how much of it was actually a joke on Chris's part. But just as how his night with Ali was none of Rick's business, this was none of his.

Thom held up his glass and eyed the level of the

amber liquid. "Staying the night here sounds damn good to me. Besides not wanting to drive after I drink this, I'm homeless until the weekend anyway. That's when the barracks manager says a room will be available."

"You're not alone, buddy. There was no room at the inn for me either. You must've got on the list before me. They told me it'd be mid-January before I got a room." Zane sniffed at the glass Rick had handed him, not looking all that concerned he was without accommodations for the next two weeks.

Jon shook his head at the ongoing housing debacle on base. "You know you can all crash at my place for as long as you need to."

"I know and thanks." Zane tipped his head. "I'll likely just rent one of those rooms by the night until my turn comes up. Unless of course, some sweet young thing asks me to crash with her for a while."

"Pfft." Thom snorted. "I don't have Zane's obvious excess of cash since all my money goes to the ex-wife and I don't want anything to do with any sweet young things—also thanks to my ex-wife—so I'd be happy to take you up on your generous offer, Jon. You're a lifesaver."

"Anytime."

"Okay, enough women and housing woes. You'll all stay the night tonight and I'll cook us breakfast in the morning. But now, it's time for the toast." Rick had finished passing out the glasses and stood with his raised.

Champagne glasses in their hands, Ali and Darci stood way off to the side as observers rather than participants in what had become the team's tradition a few years back.

Rick glanced around the group and when every man had his glass held aloft, he said, "To absent friends and fallen brothers."

"Absent friends and fallen brothers." Jon joined the chorus as they echoed the words, then he pressed the glass to his lips. He felt the burn all the way down his throat to his belly. He slammed the empty glass on the counter and blew out a breath. "Phew. Where's that food you promised? Another shot like that and I'll be shitty."

"Here you go." Ali moved a platter from the counter to the island.

One glance at the bite-sized foods made Jon wonder. Mini anything wasn't going to satisfy a hoard of hungry SEALs for long, but Darci had promised lasagna and he knew from all Rick's talk that she made a killer one. It had been a long time since he'd had home cooking. Jon's mouth started to water just at the thought.

"Try the mini quiches." Ali gestured toward the tray. "They're really good."

"Okay. Thanks." He grabbed the tiny pastry and popped it into his mouth, wondering if it would be rude to take like six more to hold him over.

"You're welcome." Ali sent him a smile so seductive that Jon began to salivate for a completely different reason than the food.

He was sex-deprived and riding a home-from-deployment high, but Ali could be a dangerous option to relieve his ache. He thought about her far too much considering it was supposed to have been a fling.

Rick poured another round of drinks and someone thrust one into Jon's hand. At this rate he wouldn't have to worry about making the bad decision to give in to the temptation of a repeat with Ali. He'd be passed out in front of the television in Rick's easy chair by midnight.

Jon glanced at Ali and saw the tip of her pretty pink tongue shoot out to catch the melted cheese that ran out of whatever she'd just bit into. As he realized he was standing in the middle of the party with a semi hard-on, he had to think that him being passed out cold might be a good thing.

CHAPTER TEN

Darci frowned at Ali's glass. "That's not champagne."

She laughed at the accusatory tone. "No, it's seltzer. I stopped drinking so I can drive home."

"But it's New Year's Eve."

"And the cops will be crawling all over the place."

"So stay here."

Ali laughed at that. "It looks like you're going to have a house full already."

And Ali might have been happy to be one of those overnight guests given that Jon would apparently be one also after how much scotch he'd consumed. But he had yet to speak another word to her since thanking her for passing the tray of quiche.

Now, it was minutes to midnight. Ali knew that if he'd wanted to spend the night with her, he'd already be over here sealing the deal. . . no Navy SEAL pun intended. As it was, Jon wasn't hovering nearby in preparation for a kiss at midnight.

Ali didn't need a sledgehammer to the head to tell her it wasn't happening tonight, if ever. She sure as hell wasn't going to act like some high school loser hoping the quarterback noticed her hanging around his locker.

"So you're going to leave me here?" Darci frowned deeper and shook her head. "The only female in the middle of all these guys?"

"We really don't have a lot of female friends, do we? We should probably work on that." Even the two people from Rick's work who'd shown up were men.

Darci waved that concern away. "Just stay here."

"Why don't you come home with me? That way the guys will have another bed." She glanced around at the group of large men. Rick would need the extra space to accommodate them all. Then again, maybe Darci wanted to stay here with at least one of them. "Unless you wanted to stick around here. Spend more time with the guys. You didn't get to talk to Zane much tonight."

Ali took a stab at the one guy she sensed her friend had a thing for. Darci screwed up her face at the mention of his name. "No. Do you know what Zane's been doing the whole party?"

"Besides drinking and eating and hanging out with his friends? No, I don't."

"He's been texting every girl in his phone trying to line up a booty call for tonight." Anger smoldered in Darci's eyes.

For her to be that pissed about Zane texting other women meant Ali had most likely hit the nail on the head. Darci was interested.

"Then come home with me. We'll sleep late. Tomorrow, I'll make us coffee and cinnamon rolls and we can sit around and watch home decorating shows or whatever. We can put what we want on the television with no men to bitch about it." Ali knew that the single television and control of the remote was a hot issue in this household since Rick had moved in.

Darci thought for a second. "All right. That actually sounds like a perfect morning. And it will leave Rick to tend to his friends and their hangovers all by himself. If I stay I know I'll end up cleaning the God awful mess he'll make in the kitchen when he cooks breakfast for them all."

"Good. It's a deal." Ali raised her glass to Darci's. "To our girls' day tomorrow."

"To girls' day." Darci clinked and downed the rest of her champagne. "I need a refill before midnight."

Ali watched her friend head toward the bar, before she visually searched the room for Jon. She found him standing off on the side, listening to some story Chris was telling to the group.

Jon's stare caught hers. She held it for longer than was proper for accidental eye contact. Feeling her cheeks heat, she yanked her gaze away.

"Holy shit. Look at the time. It's almost midnight." Rick's announcement pulled Ali out of wallowing in her embarrassment.

She glanced at the screen on the muted television

and saw the countdown had begun. The numbers on the screen said it was thirty seconds to midnight.

"I'm ready to toast to the end of this shitty year." Thom raised his glass.

"Your divorce. My knee surgery. I'm right there with you, man. It was a shit year." Rick held up his own short glass of liquor and Ali realized all the guys had abandoned drinking beer and settled on just the hard stuff.

"We're all on the right side of the dirt, aren't we?" Chris asked. He raised his glass to Thom and then to Rick. "Divorce and knee surgery aside, we're all standing here together, safe and whole. If this was a shit year, I hope next year is just as shitty."

"Amen to that." Darci's soft declaration came from closer to Ali than she'd expected.

Unexpectedly choked up at the words and the meaning behind them, Ali turned and clinked her glass to Darci's. "Amen."

The giant numbers had continued flashing on the television during Chris's speech until the guests echoed the countdown aloud.

". . . three, two, one." The room resonated with a deep, loud, "Happy New Year" that could only be produced by a team of men used to working together. She laughed when she got a look at the coordinated toast made by the circle of guys, shoulder to shoulder, glasses raised high as they all met in the middle.

Then the moment passed. The circle broke and there was back slapping and hand shakes for everyone.

Chris broke off from the revelry and made a beeline for Darci.

"I'm not getting screwed out of a New Year's kiss." He tipped his head toward the guys. "They're all too ugly, so it's gotta be you, darlin'."

Grinning wide, Chris reeled in Darci with one arm, dipped her deep and gave her a kiss worthy of one of those corny old black and white movies.

Ali watched, wide-eyed, from not a foot away. There was quite a lot of intrigue surrounding her. If she wasn't mistaken, Chris liked Darci, while Darci was interested in Zane. And Zane apparently wanted any girl in his phone willing to text him back for a booty call. It all felt very high school, especially when Ali's own crush stepped into her line of vision and her heart began to pound like she was a teenager again.

Jon put his glass down on the counter. "Happy New Year."

She turned to fully face him. "Happy New Year."

Not sure exactly what to do—shake his hand, kiss him on the cheek, kiss him on the lips—she waited for him to make the first move. And oh, boy, did he make one hell of a move as he palmed her face, leaned in and crashed his lips against hers.

Jon planted one hell of a kiss, dead on her mouth, while she stood there with a glass in one hand and uncertain what to do with the other. As the kiss went on for far longer than a peck, she reached blindly for him and looped the fingers of her free hand into his waistband.

Drawing in a breath through his nose, Jon moved

one leg forward to nestle his thigh between hers. Pressing closer, he thrust his tongue between her lips.

She felt ridiculous still holding her glass, but couldn't see to put it down. It didn't matter anyway. The sounds in the room permeated the private bubble Jon's kiss put her in and reminded her they were by no means alone. Feeling the erection pressing against her, she wished they were alone. But the taste of the scotch he'd been drinking was a reminder that unlike in July, tonight Jon wasn't sober.

He'd been polite and pleasant but definitely aloof all night, but now, many drinks later, he was all over her. There was nothing like some straight alcohol to make a man horny.

Ali pulled back, breaking the kiss as her mind spun for something to say.

Jon took a step back and dropped his hold on her. "I'm sorry. That was. . ."

"The holiday? The scotch? The fact you're happy to be home and alive." She smiled. "Really, Jon, it's all right."

He laughed and shook his head. "*Inappropriate* was the word I was going for, but yeah, the rest of those all apply too."

She waited. For him to ask her out. For him to suggest they go somewhere more private. For basically anything.

Jon hooked a thumb toward Rick's bedroom door. "I'm gonna go hit the head."

That was the last thing she'd expected, but she nodded. "Okay."

"What the hell was with that kiss?" Darci's voice brought her around before Jon had even cleared the doorway.

"I could ask you the same thing." Ali's brows shot high.

Darci flicked one wrist. "That's just Chris being Chris, but Jon and you? Oh my God—"

Ali held up her hand to stop Darci. "Relax. That was the result of too much scotch." She blew out a breath and looked around at all the remaining men in the room. "I've about had enough of the testosterone overload tonight. You ready to go soon?"

Darci's gaze cut to Zane, deep into texting someone. "Yeah. Definitely. Just let me throw some things in a bag. Be back in a minute."

"Sounds good." Ali nodded.

The sooner the better.

It was easy to forget when Jon's hotness was nearby and pressed against her, but Ali suspected things would go one of two ways and neither was good. She could have another fling and then spend the next months waiting and wondering if she'd ever hear from him again, or they could get involved more seriously. Then she'd have to live with all the secrecy, and his disappearing with no notice to travel who knew where to do God only knows what.

Ali knew the deal. Yes, Jon was back stateside, but that was just a change of address. If Rick's time with the unit was any example, Jon would mysteriously disappear for days or weeks at a time and come home with unexplained injuries, gunshot wounds included, only to say they were from a training accident.

He'd lie about where he was going and why. He'd be vague about how long he'd be gone. All because of a job that would always come first. Before his family. Definitely before a girlfriend, if that was even what Jon wanted Ali to be.

More likely was that Jon wanted a casual thing. Maybe that was smart, given his life. Then again, maybe he was just a man who'd take it anywhere he could get it, just like Zane appeared to be.

Jon came back into the room. His eyes cut to her before he turned toward the guys who'd settled on the sofa. Things looked like they were winding down a bit. Ali put her glass down and moved into the kitchen. She figured she could get a jump on washing the glasses and gathering up the trash so when Darci was ready they could leave the guys on their own with a clear conscious and only the leftover food—if there was any—to be put away.

The sooner she was away from the man who attracted her like he had his own gravitational pull, the better.

CHAPTER ELEVEN

"Damn, that was good." With a full belly, Jon lay on the sofa like a slug, barely rallying the energy to raise the coffee cup to his mouth. He might be unsatisfied in the sexual department, but he sure as hell wasn't lacking in food.

Rick grinned. "Well, you really can't screw up bacon and scrambled eggs, but thank you much."

"No?" Zane let out a snort. "The chow hall somehow manages to."

There was a chorus of grunts from the men as testament to that truth.

Jon, Brody and Chris lounged in their underwear, while Zane and Thom, who were temporarily sans barracks accommodations and still had their travel bags in their vehicles, wore PT shorts.

As the weather girl bounced across the screen on the television in front of a map showing the United States, Jon angled his head toward Rick.

"So what's your plans for today?" Jon eyed the mess in the kitchen, part a remainder from the party last night, part from this morning's cooking. "Besides cleaning up, I mean."

Rick shrugged. "Nothing much. I've got work tomorrow so I figured I'd just kick back today."

"I'm going to try to call the wicked witch—I mean the ex-wife—and see if I can see the kids even though it's not my scheduled day. She probably won't let me, but it's worth a try."

Chris blew out a breath. "Damn, Thom. That's tough. I'm sorry."

"My own fault. She was a bitch when I got her pregnant and married her, so how can I be surprised she's one now?" Thom shrugged.

That reality check put a damper on Jon's mood. Making a relationship work was tough enough. This life made it close to impossible.

Speaking of relationships and women. . . another memory began to emerge from the haze of last night, besides his ill-advised mini-make-out session with Ali at midnight. Jon swiveled his head toward Zane. "Hey, you ever get any responses to your booty texts last night?"

Every man in the room looked to Zane for a response. He frowned. "I don't know. Where's my phone?" He glanced around until he finally zeroed in on his pants. They were on the floor next to the sofa where he'd slept. Reaching down, he snagged them and felt in the pockets, pulling out a cell. He hit a button and let out a groan. "Mother fucker. Three texts. Dammit!"

Jon chuckled. "Oh well. You were in no shape to

drive anywhere or fuck anyone last night anyway."

Brody let out a laugh. "Who are you kidding? He would have had her pick him up."

"Hell, the lucky lady probably would have offered to pay a cab to come get him. For a sex god like Zane Alexander, just returned from six months away, nothing is too much." Chris grinned.

"And I assure you, drunk or sober, I can always fuck." Zane delivered that declaration with a raise of his coffee mug.

"Hey, guys. Look at this." Rick reached for the remote control on the coffee table and raised the volume on the television as a breaking news bulletin came on.

Video of a passenger plane on a runway filled the screen. Emergency vehicles, kept at a safe distance, surrounded the aircraft.

A broadcaster off-screen explained the situation, but Jon didn't need to listen. The headline at the bottom of the screen told him all he needed to know.

Hostage Situation in Ethiopia

With a sigh, he pulled his feet off the ottoman and planted them on the floor. "Oh, well. That day off was fun while it lasted. Thanks for everything, Rick."

"Fuck." Zane hoisted himself off the sofa.

Thom groaned. "Frigging New Year's Day? Couldn't these bastards have chosen January second instead?"

As Chris and Brody stood, Chris reached for his jeans and laughed. "Y'all are gonna have a fun day."

While buttoning his jeans, Brody frowned at the jumble of boots and sneakers littering the floor, no doubt searching for his. "We gotta get home quick so I can get cleaned up before we get called in. I'm not fixin' to go into a mission needing a shower and with my mouth tasting like ass."

"I hear ya." Jon had come to the party not intending to stay the night. He needed to get back to his house to brush his own teeth and shower before the inevitable recall came. Heading into the kitchen, Jon put his coffee mug in the sink with the rest of the dirty dishes. "Sorry we can't stick around to help you clean up."

Rick's brow rose. "Yeah, I'm sure. You guys go home and do what you gotta do. And the homeless among you are welcome to use the two bathrooms here. There should be towels in both showers."

"Thanks." Thom nodded.

"Appreciate it, dude." Zane headed for one doorway while Thom aimed for the other.

After pulling on his shoes, Jon paused by the front door to glance back. "I'll see you guys very soon, I'm sure. And thanks again, Rick. Tell your sister I said thanks too."

"Will do." Rick nodded, his gaze holding Jon's. "Stay safe."

Jon nodded and delivered his usual response. "That's the plan."

~ * ~

"Ugh. There's not going to be anything on any of the regular networks except this hijacking." Ali reached for the remote control to switch to one of the cable stations.

Darci opened her mouth and shut it again.

Pausing, Ali glanced at her friend. "Do you want me to leave it on?"

"No. It's fine. Change it." Darci shook her head. "It's just after so many years, it's hard getting used to the fact I don't have to stay glued to the television when anything bad like this happens."

Realization hit Ali. "Because you thought Rick might be there."

"Yeah. Funny how his 'trainings' so often coincided with these kind of international happenings." Darci made air quotes to emphasize the word *trainings*. "But he's not there this time. He's safe and sound at home, so change it. I'm good. Try the cooking channel. Or no, the home decorating network. It's a new year. I have an itch to redecorate and have a fresh new home too."

Ali eyed Darci and then the television, which was still showing the same shot of the airplane that had been on screen for the past half hour.

"Rick's friends might be there. Guys you know." Men who Ali now knew too. She said it as much to remind herself there was good reason she and Jon couldn't give in to their attraction, as to remind Darci it was natural for her to be concerned.

"I know. I hope Zane is done with his booty call, just in case they're called in." Darci's joke rang hollow.

Ali knew Darci would worry about Zane and all the guys, no matter what she said. So would Ali, about Jon in particular.

It was an impossible situation, she and Jon. So why couldn't she get that midnight kiss out of her mind? She hit the buttons to change the channel and forced herself to be interested in the woman decorating her dining room with antique silver for a New Year's Day brunch.

A commercial break came on and changing the subject seemed like the best course of action to get both of their minds off the guys. "I can't believe we have to work tomorrow."

"I know. It sucks."

"Yup." With that topic covered, Ali needed a new one. "More coffee? Or juice?"

"I'm good. Thanks."

"Okay, well let me know if you want anything. Or just help yourself."

"All right." Darci wasn't helping much.

Ali gave up on trying to make conversation. She went back to pretending to watch the TV, but her mind wasn't on the show. Not even close.

CHAPTER TWELVE

The aircraft bounced onto the runway and Jon stretched. "Home again."

Zane lifted a brow. "Maybe this time we'll be here longer than twenty-four hours."

His butt numb from the length of time spent in the uncomfortable seat, Jon had to agree. "One can only hope."

He reached into his pocket, pulled out and turned on his phone. After a few seconds, voicemails and texts began to flood in, sending the vibrating cell into a jig in his hand. Next to him, Zane's phone did the same.

Jon frowned. "What the hell? What did we miss?"

They'd been brought in as back up for the unit stationed on the Horn of Africa, who was already on site in Ethiopia. After flying to Djibouti, Jon's unit had cooled their heels for a bit in the SEAL encampment on Camp Lemonier waiting for orders. Finally, they were brought to the airport where the hijackers held the airplane and the hostages. There they got to sit around and wait some more.

They'd been gone less than a week. Even so, it was obvious something had happened in that time.

"There's only one way to find out." Eyes on his cell, Zane started to press buttons. "Look's like the bulk of them are from Rick and they came in today."

Crap. Rick always kept in touch but he'd never blow up Jon's phone with messages when he knew they were gone. Not like this. Not even when some pretty important shit had happened in his life, like when he'd gotten hired at his new job and when he'd finally gotten a call from the girl he'd given his number to.

"Something must be wrong." The texts all said basically the same thing in different variations. *Call.* Jon moved on to the voicemails, hoping they might yield a clue.

"Hey, y'all get a shit ton of messages?" Brody leaned over from his seat.

"From Rick? Yeah." Zane continued to scroll through his texts as Jon pressed his phone to his ear to listen to the voicemail.

"Not just Rick." Brody shook his head. "Chris texted more than once telling me to call him ASAP. Something must've happened."

Jon nodded. There was no other conclusion he could come up with based on the evidence.

Yeah, in past when anything huge happened in the world—such as the taking out of Osama Bin

Laden—Jon had gotten a bunch of messages from anyone and everyone who knew what he did for a living. Everyone assumed he'd been on that mission. The truth was, he'd been training in Mississippi at the time. Not that it mattered. He would have told everyone he wasn't there, that he'd been training, even if it weren't true.

This mission hadn't been anything like that. It wasn't even like the high profile rescue of Captain Phillips from Somali pirates that Jon had actually been on, which had also yielded a bunch of texts, calls and emails.

This mission, the hijacking in Ethiopia, was small potatoes in comparison. One shot had been fired, and it hadn't been by Jon, but rather by one of the guys in the unit currently stationed in HOA. The head hijacker had given them a clear shot when he dragged a hostage to the open main cabin door of the aircraft. The mistake cost him his life. After that, the rest of the hijackers had come out with their hands up.

Yes, it had probably all played out on television, as much as they'd tried to keep the news crews away, but it shouldn't have garnered this kind of response, and not from seasoned operatives like Rick and Chris.

A feeling of sickness settled in his gut as the voicemail message came on and Rick's panicked voice filled his ear.

"I'm trying all of you guys even though I know damn well you won't get this if you're still on the mission or in the air. Fuck! I don't know what else to do. Just call me when you can. Please."

Something was wrong but Jon still didn't know what. Giving up on the messages, he hit the button to dial. "I'm calling Rick now."

Brody nodded, focusing on his own cell. "I'll hit up Chris and see what I find out."

Rick answered Jon's call on the first ring. "Jon. Thank God."

"We just touched down and got your messages. What's wrong?"

"It's Darci. And God, Jon, Ali too. He's got them locked in the bank."

Fighting his own reaction, Jon said, "All right, Rick. Slow down and give me the SITREP. Who has them locked in the bank?"

Rick drew in a loud, shaky breath. "Okay. A witness outside the bank saw a masked man carrying an automatic weapon walk into the building at approximately eleven-hundred. She called 9-1-1. He's locked three bank employees inside with an unknown number of customers."

Jon glanced at the time. Ali and Darci had been hostages for more than three hours.

"So one hostage-taker and at least three, possibly more hostages?"

"Yeah. The news says that a couple of the bank employees had gone on break right before the gunmen walked in. Christ, I wish it had been Darci."

"I know, Rick. Keep it together, man. Everyone's going to be fine." Jon had to believe that himself. "Are the authorities in phone contact?"

"I don't think so. They have a negotiator on a bullhorn trying to convince him to release at least the women. That's all I know. I'm behind the police barricade with the rest of the civilians and press."

"Did you tell them your sister is in there?"

"Yes, of course. They don't give a shit." Rick's frustration was clear in his voice.

The police wouldn't want any collateral damage if things went bad, but Jon understood Rick's feelings perfectly. He just couldn't let his association with Darci or Ali cloud his thinking. Jon moved on to trying to find a motive for the situation. "Has the gunman claimed affiliation with any organization?"

"No. I don't think so. Not yet. They haven't mentioned it on the news if he has."

That was strange. He'd figure a man risking his life to take a bunch of bank employees hostage would want to shout about why he was doing it.

Rick drew in a breath and continued, "But who the hell knows for sure? I'm getting more information from the internet than the authorities on site at this point."

"What've they got there? How are the police set up?" Jon asked Rick something he would be able to answer.

"Not just police. A few suits just showed up that have the look of Feds to them. I'd say close to sixty men, which includes uniformed police, S.W.A.T., tactical support units and the suits I mentioned. Squad cars blocking the roads. I see one, two, three snipers on surrounding rooftops."

"What's the layout of the bank building?"

"Glass entrance foyer on the south side. Double sets of doors leading into the lobby area with the tellers' counter. Drive up window, north side. Offices off to the east side with windows in the front. No windows or visibility on the west side of the building."

By now every member of Jon's unit was up and out of their seats and clustered around him, listening to his side of the conversation. He resisted the urge to hit speakerphone. The others on the flight didn't need to be privy to all that was happening.

"Where is he holding the hostages?" He kept his voice down while reaching to release his safety belt. The Air Force crew would lower the ramp any minute and the crew chief would give the order to disembark.

"From what I've overheard, they think they're in the vault."

"Location?"

"North-east side of the building."

Jon pictured the building in his mind. "How many stories?"

"One."

That was good news. The roof could be the weak point. A team, choppered in, could fast rope down and at least place a listening device so they could hear the state the hostages were in.

The hostages. . . Jon had to objectively think of them as faceless, nameless, but they weren't. He knew at least two of their names, and he knew a lot more about Ali than just her face. And Darci—he could only imagine what Rick was feeling right now.

Jon wrestled his focus back to where it needed to be. "They have anyone on the roof yet?"

"No, but that's what I would do if it were up to me." Rick let out a sigh. "These S.W.A.T. guys— Jon, I've seen them work in this kind of situation. They go in guns blazing. It's amazing the hostages aren't killed right along with the hostage-takers."

Talking logistics had seemed to bring Rick back to his years of training and put him in work mode. He'd sounded calmer for a bit, but now the panic returned to his voice when he talked about the possibility of casualties.

He knew Rick would feel better to be doing something rather than cooling his heels. So would Jon, and maybe there was something he could do about that. "We're getting off the transport now. I'll get there as soon as I can, but listen. If there is any chance, even a suspicion that this guy is a foreign terrorist, or even an American with ties to Al Qaeda, they could bring us in."

"I hear ya. Let me see what I find. I'll call you back."

Rick sounded more hopeful before he'd disconnected. Jon giving him a task, and some hope, had helped.

Jon lowered his cell and glanced around him. "You guys hear all that?"

Brody dipped his head in a nod. "Yeah, and Chris filled me in on what he knew. He's on site with Rick."

Jon checked the time again and blew out a breath. "It's coming up on four hours since he locked down the building."

Anything could have happened inside that bank during that time and the authorities might know

110

nothing about it.

Zane cocked a brow. "Jon, you know how these things go. It's all sit around and wait. If he'd killed a hostage, he'd have announced it somehow to prove he's serious."

Jon nodded. Zane was right. They all knew how these things went. They'd just experienced it in Ethiopia. The only difference was that there everyone was waiting around staring at a jet instead of a bank.

Dammit, how long before they could get off this damn transport? Jon glanced at the front and then back to his guys. "If we can find out something to convince headquarters that this guy has terrorist affiliations, we might be able to get in there. Otherwise. . ."

"We'll be sitting on the sidelines as spectators right along with everyone else." Grant finished Jon's sentence.

"Chris and Rick are there doing what they can until we check in at base and can get over there."

Brody was right. First things first, but Chris and Rick weren't an advance team. They were civilians. And Jon's unit had no jurisdiction. Even if they could wrangle proving that they should, they'd still have wait for orders to come down from command.

Until then, Jon was next to powerless to help and it was frustrating as hell. All of his training was for shit if he wasn't allowed to use it when he needed to.

With the image of Ali's face in mind, Jon imagined how frightened she must be. The thought nearly immobilized him.

Just make it off the aircraft and check in. He'd move on to the next milestone from there. One thing at a time.

He reached for his backpack as the exit finally opened.

~ * ~

"What language is that?" Ali hissed the question as softly as she could and still have Darci hear her.

They sat on the floor of the bank's vault, along with the loan manager and the customer who'd been unlucky enough to decide to do his banking today.

Eyes on the gunman, Darci answered, "Some sort of Arabic, I think."

They all watched as he paced and spoke rapidly into the biggest cell phone Ali had ever seen.

"Do you think he can't speak English? That's why he's not answering the phone or making demands?"

Darci shrugged. "Maybe."

The customer, a burly man who was dressed like some sort of construction worker, glanced at Ali. "Sounds like Pashto."

Ali's gaze shot to the man. "How do you know?"

"Served two tours in Afghanistan before I got out."

"Can you speak it?"

"A few words, but I heard it spoken enough to recognize it."

Ali's mind spun with what to do with this information. Keeping her eyes on their captor, Ali asked Darci, "Do you think Rick can speak it?"

"I don't know. Maybe. Probably. A little." Darci's eyes widened. "Why? You're not planning on trying to talk to this crazy guy, are you?"

"If we could communicate enough to convince him to let us call your brother, he could tell Rick what he wants. . . We have to open communications." Ali watched the gunman looking more and more agitated as the moments went on.

So far his obsession with making phone calls to whoever was probably pulling the strings of this operation had worked in their favor. They were basically left to themselves in the vault. But for how long?

Milton Hamilton, the bank's loan officer and probably twenty years Ali's senior, shook his head. "I think we need to lay low. It seems like he's pretty much forgotten about us."

"For now. That might not be the case for long. Besides, I don't wanna be here when he gets the order from above to detonate that vest he's wearing. They could be waiting to do it live on the evening news for all we know."

Ali glanced at the thickness of the open vault door before directing her attention to Milt and the customer. "Will this door, this whole vault, withstand the blast of that thing he's wearing?"

"Probably. If we could get it closed in time," Milt answered. The door swung out rather than in, making it all the more difficult for them to reach it and close it.

"That'll only work if he's not in here with us when he blows it." The customer's added observation deflated Ali's plan further.

The gunman turned to glare at them, putting a halt to the hushed conversation for a few minutes until he started pacing again while yelling into his cell.

The office phone rang on Milt's desk right outside the vault, as it had on and off for Ali wasn't sure how many hours. That, in combination with the noise of the buzzing, ringing and singing pile of cell phones the gunman had collected from them and tossed on the desk before shoving them into the vault, was enough to drive anyone crazy—a realization that particularly disturbed Ali given the suicide vest strapped onto their captor.

She shook her head, searching for something to do rather than what they had been doing, which was nothing. "I still think if the police spoke to him in his own language it would help."

Darci cocked a brow. "But there's no way to get that news to them, now is there?"

"I have a cell phone."

Ali pivoted toward the customer. "What?"

"I only gave up the cell my boss gives me to use for work. I still have my personal one."

Her eyes widened. "What should we do? Call 9-1-1?"

Milt shook his head, while staring at the gunman. "We can't call. He'll hear."

"We can text. Darci, text Rick. He'll know what to do." Ali turned to the man who might possibly be their savior. "What's your name?"

"Tim."

"Tim, can you send a text without him seeing?"

"Yeah, I think so. Signal in here's crap though." Tim glanced down at the phone. "I'm getting one—now two bars."

"Try. A text might get out even if the signal's not strong." Pieces of Ali's plan began to come together. "Make sure it's on silent."

"Already is. So who do I text?" Tim raised a brow and glanced at Darci.

She whispered Rick's cell number as Tim entered it, shielding the cell on the floor from view with his body.

"What are you going to say?" Milt asked.

"He'll need to know where we're located in case they come in shooting. And say what kind of firepower he's got." Being the sister of a SEAL for all those years had apparently rubbed off on Darci. She supplied information that Ali wouldn't have thought of herself. At least not in her current state.

"All right. One gunman. Speaking Pashto on satellite phone," Tim whispered as he typed the text into the cell.

"That's good." Darci nodded. "It will tell them he's got a boss or partner somewhere off site."

Probably Al Qaeda. Ali kept that cheery thought to herself while Tim continued typing as he whispered, "Suicide vest, one automatic weapon. Four hostages in vault."

"Good. Sign it *Darci*, spelled with an 'i' so he knows it's us," Ali added.

"Yeah," Darci agreed. "He won't recognize your number."

"Okay. Sent." Tim blew out a breath and slipped the phone into one of the pockets in the leg of his cargo pants.

Ali mirrored Tim's exhale and glanced again at the man, looking more upset as the moments passed.

Milton too glanced at the gunman who was the center of everyone's attention. "Let's hope it helps."

There wasn't much left to do but hope and pray. With everything in her Ali did both, asking whatever power might be listening to make sure that Rick was out there reading that text right now. If Jon and his SEAL buddies could be there too, that would be even better.

CHAPTER THIRTEEN

"I don't like being helpless." Jaw set, his eyes never leaving the building where his sister was hostage, Rick's nostrils flared as he drew in a breath.

"I know the feeling." Jon had been experiencing it far too much lately. All of his training and experience didn't mean shit if he wasn't allowed to use it.

Between the government trying to make it look to the world as if everyone in Afghanistan would play nicely together if the military just asked politely enough, and this situation where he and his team of the most highly trained operatives in the United States Navy were being kept behind a police blockade, Jon was ready to blow.

"It'll be okay, man." Zane eyed the building as well, his gaze moving to the snipers on the roof.

Rick shook his head. "I'm not so sure."

"Sure, it will. Y'all will see. Before you know it we'll be back at your place sipping on scotch to celebrate." Chris shot Jon a look that showed his concern even as he reached out and squeezed the back of Rick's neck.

"Who the hell is texting me now?" Frowning, Rick reached into his pocket.

"Your parents?" Chris suggested. "This shit is probably all over the news."

"No. Mom and Dad are on a cruise. I couldn't call them even if I wanted to—which I don't. Not until I have something concrete to report."

Jon hoped the definitive news Rick was waiting to report would be the safe rescue of all the hostages, Darci and Ali included.

Rick glanced down at his cell and his eyes opened wide. "Holy shit. It's not her number, but it's from Darci. Listen to this. *One gunman. Speaking Pashto on satellite phone. Suicide vest, one automatic weapon. Four hostages in vault.*"

Jon moved closer to listen as Rick read the contents of the text aloud.

Suicide vest. Pashto. Satellite phone. This was no ordinary bank robbery. Men interested in getting away with bags of cash didn't strap bombs to themselves.

Jon let out a long low whistle. "Judging by that evidence it sounds like a possible terrorist to me."

A smile spread across Chris's face. "I reckon it does, boys."

Zane grinned. "Seems to me that would put this situation right smack in our jurisdiction, no?"

"I do believe it might." Jon already had his

phone out as he glanced at Chris. "I'm calling your brother on base."

Chris let out a short laugh. "If anyone can convince the command to do what we want them to, it'll be him."

Brody, Tom and Grant had stayed at the base to take care of all the work that needed doing upon the return from the Ethiopia mission. The shit that the rest of the team had bailed on to go be with Rick. Brody could try and rally support from command.

"SITREP?" Brody answered the phone on the first ring, not bothering with hello.

"Oh, I got one hell of a situation report for ya." Jon relayed what they'd learned. He had to pull the phone away from his head as Brody whooped in his ear, before he disconnected to go talk to command.

Yeah, they were celebrating because this new information meant they might be able to do something about the situation, but it wasn't exactly good news.

What they had was a possible radical Muslim extremist armed and wearing a suicide vest, taking orders from God only knew who by phone while locked inside a building with four innocents. They had to move fast before whoever was on the other end of that phone pushed the detonator on this jihad.

This revelation changed the situation drastically. The police hostage negotiator wasn't working with some disgruntled customer pissed about mortgage rates or a foreclosure. There was no hope of talking this guy into giving himself up. He was prepared to die for whatever his cause was.

He hadn't responded to them yelling at him for

hours. There was no hope of negotiations. If the terrorists had wanted to make demands, they would have done so already, and they would have sent an English-speaking hostage-taker.

Nope. This situation called for quick, precise action. Exactly what Jon's crew trained for.

Now, all they needed to do was convince someone with some authority of that.

"Do I tell the commander on the scene about this or wait for word? You're active duty. This is your call." Rick glanced from Jon to Zane.

Jon answered first. "I say we wait for Brody to call back."

"Agreed. We keep this info under our hats until command gets back to us." Zane let out a snort. "Let's hope some *hero* doesn't take a shot and blow the vest in the meantime."

"All right, so we wait for word to come down. If it's a negative, then we'll move on to other options." What other options that might be, Jon had no clue. He eyed Rick. "That okay with you?"

"Yeah." Rick drew in a deep breath. "I hope for once command decides things sooner rather than later."

In a clear case of be-careful-what-you-wish-for, the cell in Jon's hand buzzed and Brody's name came up. A decision that fast might not be good news. When the military took action, they generally thought about it for far too long first.

Crap. Hoping he was wrong, Jon answered, "Yeah?"

"No go." The anger was clear in Brody's tone. "They say given the location has already been cleared and the chance of outside casualties minimized, and the small number of hostages inside—none of whom are high profile—the tactical teams currently on site are sufficient."

"Fucking bastards." Jon breathed the curse to himself, but of course Rick heard and understood what it meant.

Wearing an expression of dazed resolve, Rick let out a breathy laugh and shook his head. "Unbelievable."

Chris moved to Rick and laid a hand on his shoulder. "She said they're in the vault. That's the best place to be if it detonates."

Eyes still on the building, Rick shook his head. "Not if it explodes inside the vault with them."

What could Jon say to that? Rick was right. There wouldn't even be enough pieces to bury if that happened. He swallowed hard as regret filled him faster than he could deal with it.

Why the hell had he denied himself getting to know Ali better? He could have kept it casual while he was in Jalalabad. Just emails, maybe the occasional phone call or video call.

And on New Year's Eve he should have scooped her up and made love to her until the sun came up. Then spent the morning with her doing it all over again. . . Until he got recalled for the hijacking. Just as he'd gotten called in early to deploy the day he'd met her in July. His reasoning for not getting serious with her crept back through the regret.

There had to be a balance between work and personal life. Thom and his ex-wife obviously hadn't found it. Had Grant? He seemed happy, but he was still kind of a newlywed, so that had yet to be proven.

If there was a way to make it work, Jon wouldn't mind exploring it with Ali.

Now it might be too late.

"Fuck. What's going on?" Zane's question brought Jon's attention back to the situation.

A civilian dressed in Muslim garb was being brought through the police lines.

"That's the guy who works in the twenty-four hour market on the corner," Rick answered.

"What the fuck are they doing?" Jon frowned as they handed him the megaphone. "Making him the interpreter?"

Chris watched the action. "Someone must have called and told the police the hostage-taker wasn't speaking English."

Someone probably being the very command who'd refused to let Jon's unit—or hell, any unit available from Dam Neck or even Little Creek—step in.

"That's crazy. He could be saying anything to the gunman, and they won't know." Rick's panic visibly rose. "Hell, he could be an accomplice."

It was true. Jon knew a few words and phrases but not enough to interpret the fast amplified babble now spewing from the megaphone.

"Shh. Let me listen." Zane was the most proficient in the language. "*They know who you are. Put down your weapons and come out with your hands up.*"

"What happened to stalling? Asking for his demands? Calming him down? Trying to convince him to release the hostages?" Tangling his hands in his hair as if he was ready to tear it out, Rick looked ready to crawl out of his skin.

Jon had to fight the urge to rip the megaphone from the hands of the ad hoc interpreter who was fouling everything up.

"We got more worries, boys." Chris tipped his chin towards the sidewalk. "They're moving in with an assault team."

Off to the side of the entrance, out of view of the bank windows, well armed black-clad men were stacking up.

Before Jon could react, the point man blew out the bank's front glass and the S.W.A.T. team rushed forward. The sound of automatic weapon fire was fast obliterated by a blast that rocked the building.

Debris both large and small reached where they stood all the way across the street.

As police and civilians alike ducked for cover, Rick took off toward the explosion, which meant Jon, Zane and Chris were right behind him.

In the post-blast confusion, it took the guys in charge a few seconds to notice them running in. Then they were on the megaphone calling them back.

"His sister is inside!" Chris shouted over his shoulder as he ran side-by-side with Jon. It felt like it had on so many missions before Chris had retired—them running together, toward the danger rather than away from it.

Zane glanced at the police as he moved toward the other side of the street. "If they fucking shoot at us, I'm going to be really pissed."

It would be pretty ironic to survive all they had, only to be gunned down by the good guys in the street of their own town. The dust and smoke from the blast hung in the air and obscured Jon's vision, but there was no sound of weapon fire.

Jon came to a halt outside the building, wanting to see where the tactical team inside was before adrenaline and jumpy nerves had them shooting at anything or anyone who came upon them—*if* anyone was still alive and conscious after being so close to that blast.

"Darci!" Rick did not stop like Jon did. He plowed through the smoke and rubble.

"Fuck." Jon hesitated barely a second before he followed Rick in.

Rick seemed to know where he was going so Jon followed. He heard Zane and Chris shouting for medics. The assault team must be down, but still alive.

"She said they were in the vault." Rick skidded to a stop and reached for the vault's massive door mechanism.

Jon internalized the significance of the fact that the vault door was closed and intact. The bomb had obviously blown out in the lobby of the bank, which meant the hostages could be fine, having been shielded from the impact of the blast.

Rick yanked on the handle and the door swung open. In seconds, Darci and Ali spilled out. There were two men inside as well, but Jon couldn't drag his eyes off Ali. The sheer relief at the sight of her nearly took him off his feet.

"Oh my God." Rick enveloped Darci in a hug.

"Are you okay?"

"I'm fine."

Jon took a step forward to where Ali stood, shell-shocked, teary-eyed, and the most wonderful thing he'd ever seen. "Are you hurt?"

She shook her head but didn't speak. She was shaking so badly she was vibrating. He reached out and pulled her against him, wrapping both arms around her and squeezing tight. "Thank God you're okay."

"We closed the door." The simple statement was muffled against his chest, but at least she was talking.

He forced out a laugh. "I saw. Good job." What he didn't add was that it might have saved their lives.

Ali glanced up at him. "We heard shots." She was speaking much more loudly than she should be. Her ears would be ringing for a while as a result of the blast. "Tim closed the door just as we heard the bomb go off."

Jesus, they'd just gotten it shut in time. Jon pushed that thought out of his mind. What ifs didn't matter now. She was safe.

"I'm going to have to congratulate Tim. He's a real hero."

Thank God for whoever this Tim guy was. Though deep down Jon felt a little jealousy rise up. He hated that a stranger had saved Ali because he wasn't able to.

No, that was wrong. He was *able*, but he hadn't been allowed to. The anger rose again. Jon tamped it down. "Come on. Let's get out of here. All this dust isn't good for your lungs."

He dropped his hold on her but she continued clinging to him with both arms. That was fine with him. Wrapping one arm around her shoulders, he turned them toward the exit and the devastation. He shielded her face with one hand so she wouldn't see the gruesome damage that blast she'd so narrowly escaped had wrought.

"The EMTs are going to want to check you out." He tried to get a look at her pupils to make sure they weren't dilated, which would indicate a possible concussion, but her head remained pressed against his chest.

"I'm fine." Again, she nearly shouted the response, proving the vault hadn't completely protected those inside from all effects of the blast.

"Let them do it anyway. Okay?" He squeezed her shoulder tighter.

"Then you'll take me home?" Those big, soulful eyes he wouldn't mind staring into for hours met his. After taking note that her pupils looked normal, Jon began to allow himself to stop worrying about her.

He nodded. "Then I'll take you home."

This time he had no intention of leaving.

CHAPTER FOURTEEN

The cell phone vibrated in Jon's pants pocket.

He hopped off the sofa where he'd been watching some cartoon on the television with the volume turned all the way down and moved toward the open bedroom door. Ali was still motionless beneath the covers.

Jon pulled the bedroom door closed before hitting the button to answer the call. "Hey, Rick. How's Darci doing?"

"Eh, she'll be fine. I personally think she's kind of excited to have a war story of her own after watching us have all the excitement for all these years."

Jon laughed. "Could be."

"Where are you now? Home?" Rick asked.

He'd moved to the kitchen and was currently searching for sustenance. "Nah. I'm at Ali's place. She's still sleeping and I didn't want to leave."

He didn't want her waking up in a panic in an empty house. After the living nightmare she'd been through, there was a good chance she'd be haunted by bad dreams or wake up disoriented.

"Yeah, Darci's wiped too. Christ, Jon. I could have lost her. I still can't wrap my head around that."

Neither could Jon, one reason why he'd tucked Ali into bed last night and held her until she'd fallen asleep. Then he'd stayed, watching her sleep for hours before dozing himself. This morning, as she slept on, he finally let himself leave the room.

Rude though it might be to go through her kitchen to scavenge for food, he hadn't eaten since before boarding the transport the day before and he was starving. He spotted a box of some kind of cereal he'd never eaten before and reached for it.

Bacon and eggs would have been his preference, but he didn't want to go overboard while helping himself uninvited. Figuring cold cereal would have to do, he poured a bowl full and splashed in milk from the carton in the fridge.

Jon quietly opened drawers until he found a spoon. He dug in. . . and wrinkled his nose when it tasted like he was chewing on hay. Something that was that bad had to be healthy, so he figured at least he wouldn't starve until he got something decent to eat.

"You been watching the news?" Rick asked.

"No. I've been avoiding it. It'd only piss me off more."

Rick snorted out a laugh. "Yeah, no kidding. Two of the assault team are in critical condition.

Jon shook his head. "They're lucky they're not dead, the way they went in there like that, guns blazing. Christ. . ."

"I know." Rick's silence after those two solemnly spoken words told Jon they were both thinking the same—all the survivors were lucky to be alive.

The only casualty had been the hostage-taker, and he'd taken with him the reason why he'd been there.

Jon's team, well-trained specifically in hostage rescue missions, would have done things so differently. Knowing the hostage-taker was talking to someone on the phone, they could have put men on the roof with listening devices to monitor what was being said. Once they'd been privy to his goals, his plans, and his timeline, they could have decided the next course of action. They might have been able to take him out without the vest exploding. Hell, they might have even been able to take him alive. Gotten that all important information of who was behind this and if there were more events like it planned.

Now, all they had was a dead hostage-taker, a destroyed building, a critically injured S.W.A.T. team, four traumatized civilians, and no answers. Not to mention a juicy story for the media to speculate on and manipulate to their liking.

"God, I'm tired." Jon let out a sigh.

"So go lie down."

"No, I don't mean I need to sleep." Even though he did. "I mean I'm tired of the bullshit. We should have been sent in there. If not us, then one of the other teams."

"I know. Preaching to the choir, dude. But there's nothing any of us can do about it."

"Isn't there?" The solution came to Jon like a light being turned on overhead.

"What are you talking about? As long as you're under their command, you follow their rules."

"Exactly." Jon nodded, his pulse racing as an idea formed. "I don't want to leave while she's sleeping but after Ali is awake, I want to call a meeting."

"What kind of meeting?" Rick asked.

"A team meeting." Jon smiled as he said it, liking this idea more and more.

"Uh, I'm not on the team anymore. Remember?"

Jon shook his head. "For this, that won't matter. How about we all plan to meet today, noon, at the bar. I'll contact the rest of the guys."

"All right. Call me intrigued. I'll be there."

"You'd better be there. I'm gonna text the guys, and then go check on Ali. See you later."

"Later."

Jon disconnected that call and then wrote a single group text to Brody, Chris, Zane, Thom and Grant.

I need to talk. Can you all meet at the bar at noon?

He hit send and then powered through the remainder of the cereal. While he worked to chew through each fibrous mouthful, the responses came back. He had to hand it to the guys, not one asked why and not one said no.

These men always had his back. He hoped they'd

agree to continue to do so after he told them his idea.

Finally finished with the torturous breakfast, he rinsed the bowl and spoon he'd used and stuck them in the dishwasher. Satisfied he'd left the kitchen as clean as he found it, he crept back to Ali's bedroom door and pushed it open just a crack.

"I'm awake."

Jon opened the door wider and took a step into the room. "I'm sorry I woke you."

He'd left the bathroom light on as a nightlight in case she woke up disoriented during the night, so he saw her now as she sat up. "No, it's fine. I'd rather be awake. I've been drifting in and out in that state where it's hard to tell what's real and what's a dream. I kept thinking I was still there. . ."

That she'd had to go through that tore him up inside. He moved to the bed and sat on the edge of the mattress. "Is there someone you need to call to tell you're all right? Family?"

Ali shook her head. "My parents are in Florida so I doubt they saw it on the news. I'll call them in a little while. I'm not sure I'm up to it right now.

"Okay. You hungry?"

She shrugged. "Maybe after I wake up a little more I will be. I wouldn't mind some hot tea though."

Ali flipped the covers back, as Jon stopped her with a hand on her arm. "No, stay. I can manage to make you a cup of tea."

She shook her head. "I wanna get up."

"Okay." He rose from the bed. She swung her feet over the edge of the mattress and stood gingerly, took one step across the floor and stopped. Jon moved to stand next to her, ready to support her if she fell. "Are you dizzy?"

"No. Just stiff from sitting on the hard floor for all those hours, and then from being in bed for so long." She glanced at the morning light filtering through the closed window blinds and then at him. "You stayed all night?"

"Yup."

"You didn't have to do that."

"I wanted to."

She laughed. "Okay."

"What's so funny?" he asked.

"There was a night I wished you'd stay and you didn't. And then last night, while I'm out like a light, you stay?" Ali shook her head. "I just find that funny."

"Ali, if you hadn't been nearly blown up, there's nothing that would have kept me off you last night. I'm sorry if that's crude or inappropriate, but it's true."

She had no idea how true his words were. Not only because it had been a long time since Jon had slaked that particular hunger, but mainly because he'd almost lost her yesterday. That near miss had awakened a feral urge inside him to claim her, make her his. Lying above her, plunging inside her, feeling her writhe beneath him would have been a far better way for him to satisfy the need to possess and protect, than watching her sleep and making her tea.

She pursed her lips but didn't speak. Instead she led the way to the kitchen and Jon followed. He let her fill the teakettle herself, even though every instinct in him wanted to make her sit down so he could do it for her.

"You know all those reasons you listed in July that made it stupid for us to be anything but a one night fling?" She eyed him where he sat at the small table, watching her move around the kitchen.

He nodded. "Yeah."

"Those reasons are all still valid. You still get called away all the time, sometimes for months at a time. You still need your head one hundred percent on your job and not clouded by a relationship. Nothing's changed."

"Maybe. Maybe not." Jon wobbled his head.

He wasn't trying to be coy, but he had a lot to think about, and his crazy seed of an idea needed the buy-in of a lot of other men before it could become a reality.

She set the kettle on the burner and turned to face him. "Jon, I could have died yesterday. My ears are ringing. I feel like I could sleep another twelve hours and it still not be enough to make my limbs stop feeling like they're made of lead. You're going to have to spell things out for me here because I'm in no shape to guess what you mean."

He stood and moved around the table to pin her between his body and the counter. "I know you could have died and I'm sorry that's what it took for me to realize I want you as a part of my life. And no, nothing's changed yet, except for me and how I feel. I want to try to make this thing between us work, and when I set my mind to something, I usually don't rest until I make it happen."

A small smile tipped up the corners of her mouth. "All right."

"All right what?"

She rested her hands on his chest, before moving them around to his back. "We'll give this a try. Whatever it is."

He cupped her face in his hands. "We're gonna start with us going on a real date as soon as you're up to it."

She raised her gaze to meet his. "I'd rather have it start with a kiss right now."

"I can do that." He covered her mouth with his, sinking in to the first of hopefully many kisses in their future together. He didn't let it go on for nearly as long as he wanted it to, in deference to the trauma Ali had been through.

When he pulled away, she raised a brow. "You know, I wouldn't mind more than a kiss."

He let out a laugh. "Believe me, neither would I. But not right now. Drink your tea. Get some food in your stomach. Then, maybe, we'll talk."

A frown creased her brow. "Talk?"

He had to smile at her persistence. "We'll talk about possibly doing more than kissing. Deal?"

"All right. Deal."

"I have a meeting with the guys at noon. It shouldn't take too long, but after that, I'll be back here. . . if that's okay with you."

A small smiled bowed her lips as she dropped a teabag into a mug. "Yeah, it's okay."

"Good. Um, you might want to rest up while I'm gone, because if you're still feeling up to more than talking when I get back, that's exactly what you're going to get. I was away for a long time, so it could get a little intense."

"Promises, promises." She smirked.

"Mm, hm. It is a promise." He moved in closer, pinning her against the counter. "And I always keep my word."

He pressed a long kiss to her lips before forcing himself to break away. "Now, I'm going to cook you something to eat, then go home to shower and change so I can meet the guys."

"You might want to stop at a store while you're out." Her gaze cut sideways to him as she reached for the steaming kettle.

By the fridge where he'd been about to grab some eggs to cook for her, he paused. "Sure. What do you need?"

"More condoms. I figure a man so long denied might need more than the two banana-flavored ones left in my nightstand from last July."

A grin he couldn't control spread across his face. "Yeah. Two's probably not going to cut it."

They'd both denied themselves this for too long. Making up for it could take all night and tomorrow as well. And God help the command if they called him back in before he had a chance to make up for lost time.

CHAPTER FIFTEEN

"So we're all here now. What's up?" Rick leaned forward and rested his forearms on the edge of the table in the back corner of the bar. At noon, the place was still pretty quiet—a good place for a meeting.

"I'm considering a change." Jon delivered the words he'd thought long and hard about, but his announcement was proving more difficult to say out loud than he'd imagined.

Zane's brows rose. "What kind of change?"

The silent stares of the men around him gave Jon a clue that they might have guessed what this change entailed, but only Zane had asked for clarification outright.

Jon drew in a breath. "Yesterday at the bank really started me thinking. We're trained to deliver precise effective action, but we spend half of our time waiting for the command to let us."

"When they're not coming up with plans to rein us in while we're doing it," Thom added.

"Exactly." Jon nodded. "I'm thinking about forming a civilian company. Contract protection work. It would mean I'd have to leave active duty. It's a gamble, and I'm probably crazy for even thinking about it, but if any one of you guys want in, as equal partners, I'd love to have you."

"Wow." Thom let out a short laugh. "It sounds great to be our own bosses, but I got kids and child support to pay. I need the benefits and the steady paycheck and the pension. Dude, I gotta go to twenty years."

"I know and I understand. Believe me. If I had anyone depending on me I wouldn't even be able to consider this." Jon's gaze cut to Chris and Rick, the two who'd already gotten out of the military to join the civilian ranks. They were his best hope for partners. "The work would likely be sporadic at first, so you guys could keep doing what you're doing and just jump in when we're hired for a job."

Chris cocked a brow. "Hell, I can do that. I'm only working at the gun shop to keep busy since I retired, but what kind of jobs are we talking here? Who do you reckon will be hiring us?"

"I'm thinking, for one, shipping companies worried about secure passage through the Gulf of Aden." Jon had spent time at the SEAL camp located on Camp Lemonier in Djibouti.

Thanks to the proximity of Somalia and Yemen, the Horn of Africa region was then, and continued to be now, a hot spot. There was a collective nod from the men around the table who'd been there with him.

Grant bobbed his head. "All the publicity for the shit that went down with the Somali pirates on the Maersk Alabama is gonna be your best advertisement."

"Yup. That's what I'm thinking." Jon nodded. "Then there could be domestic needs. Big, high profile events might need additional on-site security. We could do that. And I'm hoping after our name gets out we could be the first call when shit goes down. Kind of a quick reaction force for civilian corporations."

Zane laughed. "Big rich corporations who are willing to throw money at us for a speedy, low profile resolution."

Jon's gaze cut to Zane because of the words he had chosen. "Us?"

Zane was in the same boat Jon was as far as years in, and years left to go before they'd be eligible to retire with a full pension. Right now Jon couldn't imagine being active in his current position for another decade.

Ten years until retirement felt like it might as well be a hundred.

How long before his body wouldn't be able to take the physical abuse anymore? Before he was too slow or too tired to be sharp enough to keep both himself and his team alive? His current position was a demanding job—a young man's job—and as every new BUD/S class emerged with a crop of fresh young SEALs, Jon felt a little older.

Aside from the aging of his body, his attitude was beginning to shift. That could be more dangerous than his body eventually failing him. Where he used to be able to focus and get the job done, now his mind rebelled. He took precious seconds to question the orders, to think how he'd do it differently. Those seconds could one day get him or someone else killed.

A grin tugged on the corners of Zane's mouth. "Yeah, *us*. I'm liking this idea."

That was two. Jon looked to Rick. "What do you think?"

He dipped his head. "I'm thinking if you're okay with me keeping my job and just jumping on board for assignments when I'm needed, I'm in."

Rick, Zane and Chris were in. Including Jon, that made a team of four. Not enough for some jobs, but plenty for others.

"You make it sound real tempting. Good enough it makes it look real attractive to turn in my separation package tomorrow." Grant shook his head.

Thom coughed on his swallow of beer. "You'd get out four years shy of twenty?"

"I didn't say I was going to do it, just that he makes it look tempting." Grant laughed. "I'm too close to retirement and starting in a few months I'm moving on to be an instructor for Green Team. I won't be deploying or going on missions. They handpicked me from among the senior combat veterans to train the new operators, so I figure I can coast my last few years. I can't leave now, Jon."

Jon nodded. "I know. And I'm not expecting you to give that up."

"But. . ." Grant held up a hand. "You guys make

a go of this thing, and when I'm done in four years, I damn well expect a spot on this team."

Jon grinned. "You got it."

"I wish you guys the best of luck, but..." Brody shook his head.

"There's no pressure, Brody. I honestly never expected any of you to get out with me. I just wanted you to know the offer is open."

Brody dipped his head. "Thanks. And don't get me wrong, it's a good idea, Jon."

"It's real good." Thom nodded. "You guys better not fuck this up because I expect you to have a position waiting on me when I retire too."

"You got it." Whether they were joining him or not, the support of his friends bolstered Jon's confidence.

"By then we'll be so huge we'll have to sell franchises. Hell, we might even have to let in some of the Delta Force guys just to meet the demand." Rick laughed.

Jon let out a snort. "From your mouth to God's ears. But seriously, let's not get ahead of ourselves and start counting our jobs just yet."

"But we know there's a need. We've got the men who are qualified and trained to meet that need." Rick shrugged. "Why wouldn't we succeed?"

Jon hated to put a damper on Rick's enthusiasm, but it had to be done. "What we don't have is the start-up money to get us off the ground."

"Shit. You're right." Rick visibly deflated, slumping over the table as he scowled. "Our four-tube night vision goggles alone cost what? Sixty-five thousand dollars or something crazy like that."

Chris shook his head. "I can't go back to the standard two-tube NVGs after using four. It's like trying to see through a freaking toilet paper roll in comparison."

All the training and skills in the world did them no good without the kick ass toys the Navy Special Warfare Command provided for their counter-terrorism unit, DEVGRU. State of the art, stealth transportation. Personalized, customized weapons. Not to mention the normal everyday essentials, like body armor and low tech shit like ammo. It all added up to be the tools of their trade and it cost money. A lot of it.

The energy in the room sank, as if someone had pulled the plug on the drain in the bathtub and let all the water rush out. The worst part was, that someone had been Jon.

"We can buy some stuff as surplus." Rick looked as if he was trying to sound enthusiastic about the idea. "I've got about ten thousand in my savings I was going to use as a down payment on a place of my own. I could put it into the company."

"I've got some cash socked away for a rainy day. If we all put in whatever we can—"

"That still won't come close to what we need." Jon hated to interrupt Chris's offer with another cold dose of reality. "Just our basic gear has to cost over a hundred grand each. That times four of us. We're going to need a bank loan."

Rick snorted. "Think the bank that my sister almost got blown up for would be up for giving us a loan?"

"Maybe if they'd let us go in and save the

building instead of watching it blow. What we need is an investor. A big one." Zane offering that as a solution to the problem was no help since a big investor seemed as far a stretch as a bank loan did at this point.

"Where do you propose we find this investor?" Jon asked.

"I might know somebody." Zane's playing coy was getting on Jon's nerves.

"Oh really? Who?" Jon wouldn't be at all surprised to learn that one of Zane's main squeezes was a sugar momma, rolling around in cash when she wasn't under him.

"My father."

Jon's brows rose. "Your father has the kind of money we need?"

"Yup." Zane nodded.

Rick's eyes popped wide. "And you've never told us you're frigging rich."

"I'm not rich. He is. At least the company he owns is, and they're always looking for good investments."

"And this qualifies as a good investment?" Jon had trouble believing that.

Zane smiled. "Sure. You've got the one thing my father has always wanted, but his money could never buy."

"And that is?" It wasn't lost on Jon that they were all hanging their futures on what at the moment wasn't much more than a cocky comment from Zane.

Jon really hoped Zane said something to convince him this wasn't the craziest thing he'd ever thought of doing, and he'd done some fucked up shit.

"You've got something I'd be willing to leave for. My father wants me out. He has since the day I told him I was joining the Navy. That pissed him off so badly, I decided to try out for the SEALs. When that flipped him out even more I thought what the hell, might as well go all the way."

"So you tried out for Green Team."

"Yup." Zane nodded. "I guess we're all lucky he's only rich and not so powerful or he'd probably have gotten DEVGRU shut down by now. But for this idea, Jon, I'd leave the unit. And for that, he'll fork over a hell of a lot of dough."

Jon's gut twisted as the possible collateral damage grew. Zane was sacrificing his career for this. Now, his father's money too. If this company failed. . . "You really think we can do this?"

Zane nodded. "I do. If those assholes at Blackwater can, why can't we?"

"And do it better," Chris added.

"Damn right, we can." Rick raised his bottle.

"I guess you're right." Jon couldn't argue there. "You know, we're gonna need a name for this company of ours."

"Yup, we sure do." Rick didn't seem to have any suggestions as he lifted his beer to his lips and swallowed.

The list of needs seemed to grow with every moment. The amount of details that had to be handled was daunting. It was becoming painfully obvious to Jon that he hadn't thought much past the original idea, but just like he'd done in BUD/S, he'd take things one step at a time.

Jon drew in a breath. "Anyone have any ideas?"

"How about *we've got your six*?" Thom suggested.

"Hang on. Let me write all our ideas down." Jon grabbed a cocktail napkin and turned toward the waitress, who was standing near the table behind them. "Do you have a spare pen I can borrow?"

"Sure thing." Her wide smile said Jon could probably have whatever he wanted, but Zane had already tapped that particular keg, more than once over the years. That had been enough to keep Jon at arm's length, even before he'd met Ali.

"Thanks." He accepted her pen and started to take notes. "Okay, *we've got your six*. It's not a name but it could be part of the pitch for clients."

"It'd look kick ass printed on a T-shirt too." Rick grinned.

Chris tipped his head. "Hell, yeah, it would."

Jon had a feeling T-shirts would soon be on his To Do list. "Okay, so we agree that will be a great tagline, but we still need something to call the company. Come on, guys. What else you got?"

"Battle Ready."

"Mission Ready."

"Brothers in Arms."

"Shield Security."

"Precision Protection."

"Silent Warrior."

"All right. Slow down." Jon struggled to keep up with the ideas flying at him from every man at the table, both those joining the company and those not.

"Hey, how about something Latin?" Brody

asked.

"That would be cool." Rick nodded. "Who here knows Latin?"

"We don't need to know Latin. We have the internet." Chris held up his phone.

"Can't argue with that, dude." Rick reached into his pocket.

As Chris and Rick concentrated on their cell phones, Jon noticed Brody walk to the bar. When he returned with a cocktail napkin and a pen, he started scribbling something.

Jon tried to get a look at it, but Brody's forearm blocked his view. "What are you up to?"

Brody lifted one shoulder in a shrug. "Just an idea I had."

"Let's see." Jon reached for the napkin only to have it snatched back.

"Nope. Not 'til I'm done."

Jon was reminded of middle school as Brody wrapped his arm around his work, forming a barrier so no one could see. That, of course, only made Jon want to see it more.

"Okay, here's a good Latin name." Rick read from his phone's screen. "*Carpe diem.* Seize the day."

"Wait." Chris held up one hand. "This one's better. *Cave canem.* Beware of the dog."

"So you're calling us dogs?" Zane frowned. "Dude, no."

"Hey, here's one. How about *Deus ex machine*?" Rick glanced up.

"What's that mean?" Zane asked.

"*An improbable solution, artificially introduced*

to resolve a difficulty or untangle a dramatic plot." Rick glanced up after he'd finished reading. "That's kind of what we'll be. An improbable solution for the client's difficult problems."

"Yeah, but I'm not explaining all that every time I say our name." Zane shook his head. "We need something simple. Self explanatory."

When the name suggestions had turned toward the Latin, Jon listened and wrote down the one that wasn't ridiculous, but all while keeping half an eye on Brody and what secret project he was working on.

Finally, Brody spun the cocktail napkin to face the rest of them and slid it across the table closer to Jon. Faster than the rest, Jon reached out and snatched it up.

On it was a surprisingly well-drawn sketch of an anchor with a machine gun crossing it, flanked by big bold angel wings. He read what Brody had written below and smiled.

"Listen up, guys. What do you think of this? *Guardian Angel Protection Services—we cover your six when God's too busy.*" Jon finished reading and looked up. "That's really good, Brody."

"I got the idea from your tattoo. Angel wings... guardian angel."

Rick leaned closer and got a look at the sketch on the napkin. "Damn, Brody. Who knew you could draw like that?"

"I knew." Chris tipped his chin toward the sketch. "But to come up with a kick ass name and a slogan too? That there is a surprise."

Jon glanced at the men gathered around the table.

"Should we take a vote?"

"Yeah. I don't think we're going to come up with anything better than that. I say yea." Zane raised his hand. "All in favor of Guardian Angel?"

Chris and Rick raised their hands. When Grant and Thom didn't, Jon asked, "Guys?"

"We can't vote." Grant shook his head. "We're not part of the company."

"Yet..." Jon reminded.

"Yet." Grant smiled. "Still, we shouldn't get a vote."

"Nevertheless, I'd like your opinion." Of course, Brody had come up with it so Jon didn't need to ask his thoughts, but he was interested in Grant and Thom's thoughts.

Grant reached for the napkin and took a closer look. "It's good. It says it all."

Thom grinned. "I think it's fucking awesome."

"Okay. I'm a yea also, so that means the vote's unanimous." He glanced around the group. "That's it then. We've got our name. I propose a toast. To Guardian Angel Protection Services."

Beers raised, the group echoed Jon.

Rick grinned, adding, "To G.A.P.S. We cover the gaps in your security."

Jon smiled and wrote that on the napkin.

One hurdle down. Countless more to go. Jon turned toward Zane. "You think we can really convince your father to invest?"

"Sure. You've got a logo and a slogan. You've got the personnel and a plan. And you've got me." Zane flashed his pearly whites in a wide smile.

"That we do." Jon's heart sped as he realized he

147

was going to do this. They were going to do it together.

The blood pumped through his veins as strong as it ever had before a mission, just at the thought of this endeavor, the huge step he was about to take that would change his future.

There was someone else he wanted to make sure was a part of his future, besides his buddies and new business partners. Jon pushed the chair back from the table and stood as he suddenly couldn't wait to get back to her. "Well, guys, if you'll excuse me I have someplace I need to be."

"What the hell, dude? We both decide to leave the unit we've worked our asses off most of our careers to be part of and you're leaving?" Frowning, Zane asked, "To go where?"

"I think to go to *who* is a more accurate question." Rick grinned and glanced at Jon. "She should be home. When I left my place less than an hour ago, she and Darci were on the phone. Ali said she was going to take a bath. I guess that's how girl's celebrate not getting blown up. I myself would rather celebrate with a nice stiff one."

"Oh, I think Jon's fixin' to help Ali celebrate with a *nice stiff one* too." Chris waggled his eyebrows.

Smiling, Jon shook his head, but that was the only response he was willing to give these guys, in spite of the interested looks he was getting from every man besides Rick.

He'd let them all in on his and Ali's growing relationship eventually, but this afternoon he was feeling selfish. He wanted to keep her all to himself.

And she deserved to know his plans and how they'd affect her before these guys got to know more about her and about how her presence in Jon's life had played a role in his decision.

He wasn't exactly leaving his career for a woman, but he was leaving it so he could have a life, hopefully with her as a part of it.

CHAPTER SIXTEEN

Ali got out of the tub and dried off.

A hot bath. Her big fluffy bathrobe. Nothing to do for the rest of the day but relax. Maybe she'd crack open a bottle of wine.

Hell, she deserved it after yesterday, as much as she deserved the time off with pay her boss had given her. . . and all it took was getting taken hostage and nearly blown up.

The doorbell ringing yanked her mind away from that morbid thought while at the same time the sound startled her enough she jumped.

Her nerves were still a little jittery. The bath obviously hadn't helped that. Maybe the wine would.

Pulling the robe more closely around her, she tied the belt tighter and headed for the front door. She moved the curtains to try to see who was on the front stoop. If it was anyone other than a good friend, she wasn't going to open the door. It was bad enough that a reporter had somehow gotten her number and called. Them showing up at her door was totally unacceptable.

She needn't have worried. One look at the pick-up truck in her driveway told her who the visitor was.

Smiling, she flipped the locks and pulled the door wide. "Jon."

"Hi." His gaze raked up and down her body as he stepped inside and pushed the door closed behind him. He turned to lock it and then he was moving toward her.

"I guess I missed the bath. Too bad." He fingered one wet tendril that had escaped from the messy bun she'd captured her hair in before getting into the tub. He looked like he was feeling frisky. She liked it.

Ali smiled. "Maybe I'll take another one."

"Later." The need showing clearly in his eyes told her he had other plans for the immediate future. "Oh, I almost forgot."

He pulled a small crushed brown bag from his back pocket and handed it to her. She frowned at it. "What's this?"

Before she could open the bag, he said, "Condoms."

"Oh." Ali didn't have time to come up with a better response to that information because Jon's mouth was just a breath away from hers.

He nipped at her lips with quick kisses as he backed her across the apartment.

"Where are we going?" She had a feeling she

knew.

"To bed." He moved his hands to cup her face as they continued the slow but sure journey toward the bedroom door. "That okay?"

Brown bag still clutched in one hand while the other held onto his waist, Ali smiled. "Yup."

"Good." They reached his goal—the bedroom doorway. Jon backed her all the way to the bed, tumbled her onto the comforter and crawled onto the mattress after her. "Nice robe."

He ran his hands down her sides, pausing at the belt, but he didn't untie it. She reached for the knot herself and did him the favor of opening the belt and the sides of the robe while his eyes tracked her movements.

"Damn." He breathed the word under his breath and moved his hands beneath the robe.

She felt the heat of his big, rough palms against the bare skin of her waist.

His eyes made a sweep from where his hands rested, up to her face. "Unless I get recalled, I'm staying all night."

"All right." She nodded.

"Probably tomorrow night too."

Ali smiled. "Not a problem."

Of course, they might need to go out for more supplies, depending on the number of condoms in the brown paper bag nearby.

"After that, then maybe I'll be able to keep my hands off you long enough to take you out on that date I talked about." He leaned low, nuzzling her neck with his mouth as he moved his hands up to her breast.

"Unless you get recalled." She regretted the statement the moment it left her mouth.

At her words he pulled back, his hands stopping dead in their path. One day, Ali would learn to keep her mouth shut. The only thing she wanted right now was for Jon to make love to her and then hold her all night long afterward. And when it looked as if she was about to get exactly that, she opened her stupid mouth and ruined it all.

"About that—"

"No, it's fine." She shook her head and tried to pull him down to her again to prove she was fine with what he did, as long as she could have moments like this in between the long absences and secret missions. "I understand."

"No, you don't understand." He was stronger than she was and all her efforts to tug him back to where he'd been were fruitless. "I'm getting out."

His words stopped her struggle. As much as she wanted to kiss Jon, she wanted to hear this more. "What?"

"I'm putting in my paperwork. So is Zane, and he, Rick, Chris and I are opening our own security company." Jon paused, watching her, waiting for a reaction.

Ali had no problem giving him one as her eyes widened. "Wow. Can you do that? Just quit?"

"My current contract is up soon. Zane's too. I've been procrastinating reenlisting." He shrugged. "I don't know. Maybe deep down I knew I was ready for a change."

No more deploying. No more missions. No more secrets. Just a normal job in a security company.

He'd be able to have a normal relationship. Ali's heart raced at the possibilities. "So you'll be what? Like security guards?"

"No." Jon cringed. "Not quite like security guards."

From his expression, she guessed she might as well have compared him—one of the most elite special operatives in the US military—to a mall cop.

"Well, of course not. I didn't mean it like that. You guys are much better trained." She backpedaled to undo any damage she'd done to his pride. "But this means no more getting shot at and no more flying all over the world, right?"

"I can't quite promise you that." He made a face again and bobbed his head from side to side. "We're hoping to get work worldwide and bad guys tend to carry guns, but I can say for certain there'll be no more deploying. And I'll be my own boss instead of the Navy, so I'll choose what jobs I take."

She liked the idea of that. "That sounds wonderful, Jon. I'm really happy for you."

"So you're going to be okay with all of this? My getting out of the military and opening the company. All of it?" he asked.

Ali shrugged. "Yeah, sure. The decision's yours, of course. It's your life."

"Yes, but I'm hoping you're going to be a part of that life." Jon honestly looked uncertain as he added, "If you want. . ."

Could he really be unsure that she'd want to be with him? To be part of his life?

She could relieve his worry with one word, but it

would be so much more fun to show him too. Ali moved and he moved with her, until he was lying on his back and she straddled him.

"Yes, I definitely want." Ali leaned low, closing in on his lips as she said, "You're overdressed. I want you naked."

A smirk quirked up the corner of Jon's lips. "Yes, ma'am."

It was nice to be with a man good at following orders. Ali had a feeling she was going to enjoy it immensely.

If you enjoyed *Night with a SEAL,* please consider leaving a review. And look for Zane's story, *Saved by a SEAL,* Book 2 in the Hot SEALs series from Cat Johnson.

SAVED BY A SEAL
Hot SEALs, Book 2
Cat Johnson

Zane Alexander was born with a silver spoon in his mouth, but the rebellious bad boy traded it in for a Navy SEAL trident.

Now, Zane's teammates are depending on him to get the startup capital they need to open their security company and he's gambling on his skills at covert operations. For a million dollars, he'll fake interest in Missy Greenwood, the Senator's daughter his father wants him to date in exchange for the investment.

But when Missy is kidnapped and Zane and his team are sent to Nigeria to rescue her and the others being held, bullets as well as sparks of attraction start to fly. There's no more faking when both the danger and the emotions are all very real.

SAVED BY A SEAL
CAT JOHNSON

CHAPTER ONE EXCERPT

Zane watched as Jon strode across the bar toward him.

"Good. You're here." Jon dumped a binder on the table.

The papers inside were heavy enough to make the beer in Zane's pint slosh when it landed. Zane raised a brow as he picked up his glass. "Whatcha got there, bud?"

"That's the completed business and marketing plan, all put together." Jon pulled out a chair and sat. "Rick and Darci looked it over and then both Ali and I proofread it twice, so it should be ready to present to your father."

Grateful he'd been left out of that incredibly boring stage of this project, Zane eyed the tome. "That's all? Nothing else?"

Frowning, Jon flipped open the front cover of the binder. "I think so. Brody's artwork for the logo is in there, along with a complete company branding section. I also cited and included all the materials I used for research to back up the idea. You know, as proof there's a need for this kind of operation—" Jon glanced up, scowling as his shoulders slumped. "You're fucking with me."

"I am." Amused that Jon had finally figured it out, Zane raised his glass in a toast to his gullible friend. Apparently Jon was a little slow in detecting sarcasm.

Zane took a swallow of the brew that was already getting warm. He'd arrived early for this meeting with his current teammate and soon-to-be business partner.

Truth be told, he'd needed the drink. Zane had faced the enemy with less trepidation than he felt now on the way to see his father. . . and the enemy had been carrying automatic weapons with the intent of killing him.

His father utilized weapons that were more subtle than machine guns and explosives, but no less destructive. Zane should know. He'd been dodging his father's verbal shots for as long as he could remember.

He still had yet to figure out how his mother, bless her heart, had survived this long married to his father. By keeping her head down and remaining below the radar, most likely, while Zane had a tendency to get right in his father's face. Or he had until that day he announced he was joining the Navy and walked out with nothing but what fit in his bag.

Thank God for the trust fund his maternal grandfather had set up. Zane's father could—and had—cut him off from the family's wealth and support, but even he didn't have the power to take away the trust fund in his name or the monthly allowance it yielded him.

Not that Zane's expenses were huge—living in the bachelor barracks when not deployed was cheap—but Zane did like having nice things. Big trucks. Fast cars. Hot women. That all took a good amount of cash. More than he made from his military pay, so the check was surely welcome when it appeared in his account each month.

"Do you want to take a look at what I put together?" Jon looked a little disappointed, almost crestfallen that Zane hadn't jumped to devour the binder page-by-page.

Even with the kickass winged anchor logo and company name they'd come up with on the front of it, the binder looked too much like the schoolwork he'd always hated.

Though he supposed he would need to review the material before he met with his father later that day, it could wait.

"I will. Later." Procrastination was one of the many things Zane excelled at.

He took another sip of his beer and ignored the book Jon had nudged toward him. He'd be drinking whisky if he didn't have to get behind the wheel and leave for his drive to the capital region in an hour or so.

When Jon looked ready to crawl out of his skin,

Zane decided to relieve his friend's pain. "Look, Jon. I know you, and you are incapable of giving less than one hundred percent to anything you do. I trust you that everything I'll need is in that thing, plus some. But the truth is, it doesn't matter what's in your plan. My father is going to give us the money for this company."

Jon pursed his lips. "I wish I could be so sure."

"You can be. Trust me. When my father sees I'm willing to leave the Navy for this, he'll jump on investing as much money as we need."

GAPS—Guardian Angel Protection Services—was Jon's brainchild and it was a great idea. A company comprised of a group of men with the best training the Naval Special Warfare Development Group had to offer. As combat-seasoned SEAL operatives, they would be experienced experts-for-hire at a time when precision security was a growing need in so many areas across the globe.

With their friends and former teammates Chris and Rick already out, and with Jon and Zane's current contracts about to expire, they had a four-man team to staff GAPS out of the gate with the promise of more of their teammates joining them in a few years, if they could make a go of it.

Zane traced the tip of one finger over the letters of their tagline printed on the paper slipped beneath the clear plastic front of the binder.

We cover your six when God's too busy.

Was he covering his friend's six now or leading them down a path of fruitless hope?

Nothing was certain when it came to his father. Well, nothing except the fact that the one thing

George Zane Alexander the second could never get over was his son joining the Navy against his wishes. And Zane didn't stop there. He'd taken it one step further by trying out for the SEALs. Then, as soon as he'd proven himself, he went for DEVGRU's Green Team training and selection— the infamous *Seal Team Six* the media liked to shout about.

Even if those actually in the elite unit didn't like or want the fame the media had thrust upon them after the Bin Laden raid, Zane was indeed among the best of the best, in spite of his old man's wishes. The problem was that once he'd reached the top, there was nowhere left to go to piss off his father.

Zane saw Jon's vision for GAPS as the right opportunity at the right time.

To be able to take their skills and use them as they saw fit *and* be their own bosses—it was tempting. A dream come true.

Of course, that was only *if* Zane got through this meeting with good old George without taking a swing at the man, which is what had happened the last Christmas he'd tried going home to play at being a happy family. You don't talk bad about the troops or make disparaging remarks about the war to a man who'd watched friends get blown up. Zane clenched his jaw and pocketed the anger.

Read the rest of Zane's story in
Saved by a SEAL

ALSO BY CAT JOHNSON

Hot SEALs Series
Night with a SEAL
Saved by a SEAL
SEALed at Midnight
Kissed by a SEAL
Kindle Worlds
Game for Love: Game On
Red, Hot & Blue Series
Trey
Jack
Jimmy
Red Blooded (print-only compilation)
BB Dalton (bonus read)
Jared
Cole
Bobby
Smalltown Heat (print-only compilation)
A Few Good Men (an RHB novel)
Model Soldier (an RHB novel)
A Prince Among Men (an RHB novel)
Bull
Matt
The Commander
USMC Military Romance Series
Crossing the Line
Cinderella Liberty
Oklahoma Nights Series
One Night with a Cowboy
Two Times as Hot
Three Weeks with a Bull Rider
"Fish Out of Water" (*He's the One* anthology)
"Two for the Road" (*In a Cowboy's Bed* anthology)
Midnight Cowboys
Midnight Ride
Midnight Wrangler
Midnight Darlin'

ABOUT THE AUTHOR

A *New York Times* & *USA Today* bestselling author, Cat Johnson writes contemporary romance featuring sexy alpha heroes, men in uniform, and cowboys. Known for her unique marketing and research practices, she has sponsored pro bull riders, owns a collection of camouflage and western wear for book signings, and a fair number of her friends/book consultants wear combat or cowboy boots for a living. She writes both full length and shorter works and is contracted with Kensington and Samhain.

For more visit **CatJohnson.net**
Join the mailing list at **bit.do/CatsNews**

Made in the USA
San Bernardino, CA
23 July 2015